95 MILLION AMERICANS SUFFER FROM STRESS. QR WAS DEVELOPED FOR THEM—AND QUITE POSSIBLY FOR YOU.

"In my work with patients, I have seen QR bring relief from a wide range of physical and psychological problems including migraine headache, hypertension, pain and depression, and various types of creative 'blocks.' QR has provided an alternative to drugs that were ineffective, produced unpleasant side effects, or involved a risk of addiction . . . Like me, better than 80 percent of the people who have gone through the QR program say that QR has changed their whole attitude toward life."

—Charles F. Stroebel, M.D.

CHARLES F. STROEBEL, M.D., who developed the nationally acclaimed QR program, is Director of Research at the Institute of Living in Hartford, Connecticut, as well as Professor of Psychiatry at the University of Connecticut School of Medicine, and Lecturer in Psychiatry at the Yale University School of Medicine.

QR

THE QUIETING REFLEX

CHARLES F. STROEBEL, M.D.

BERKLEY BOOKS, NEW YORK

Grateful acknowledgment is made to the following
for permission to use previously published material:

Pergamon Press, Inc., for Social Readjustment Rating Scale, by
Holmes & Rahe, first published in *Journal of Psychosomatic Research*,
Vol. 2 (1967), pp. 213-18, copyright © 1967, Pergamon Press, Inc.

QR THE QUIETING REFLEX

A Berkley Book / published by arrangement with
G. P. Putnam's Sons

PRINTING HISTORY
G. P. Putnam's Sons edition / May 1982
Berkley edition / April 1983

Acknowledgments

Books don't just happen. They require the loving sacrifice and devotion of many teachers, colleagues, family, staff, students and especially patients, who constantly teach a physician/author to self-correct. I am indebted to Erik Peper, Ph.D., and Gay Luce, Ph.D., who first introduced me to the concept of self-regulation; to Doctors Elmer and Alyce Green and Jack Schwarz, who helped me grow in comprehending its dimensions; to my teachers at the Yale Medical School, the University of Minnesota, and The Institute of Living; and particularly to my mentor and colleague for twenty years, Bernard C. Glueck, M.D., who has been a constant source of inspiration and encouragement.

The QR concept has gained significant maturity through association with Doctor Peter Wengert, Francine Butler, Ph.D., and many close friends in the Biofeedback Society of America.

The book itself would not be a reality without editorial assistance from Jane Archer, Naomi Vogel, Denise Demong, Nancy Perlman, Linda Healey, Elaine Berman, Marcia Hayden, Mary Ann Goodell, Bonnie Szarek and Dorothy Aldridge.

Dedicated to my father and mother, who kindled and fostered a compelling curiosity about the mystery of the world around me, a gift I shall always cherish. To my sister Florence for her constant source of inspiration, and especially to my wife, Elizabeth Stroebel, and the children, Mark, Lisa, Susan, Chuck IV, and Chris.

Contents

Prologue

You may be one of ten million Americans dependent on medications, either prescribed or available across the drugstore counter, for regulation of one of the symptoms listed below.

Tension Headache	Cold Feet	Nausea
Migraine Headache	Burping	Excessive Sweating
Jaw Clenching	Gassiness	Sexual Worries
High Blood Pressure	Acid Stomach	Performance
Low Back Pain	Palpitations	Anxiety
Constipation	Restless Body	Feelings of Anxiety
Diarrhea	or Legs	Feelings of Tension
Cold Hands	Butterflies in	Feelings of
	Stomach	Irritability
		Sleeping
		Difficulties

Or you may be one of 95 million Americans experiencing one or more of these symptoms, and, as such, a potential candidate for overuse of medicines such as minor tranquilizers, antacid suspensions or pills, painkillers, sleeping pills, cold remedies, laxatives, or alcohol-based syrups.

In the pages that follow, you will learn why taking drugs for these conditions may be defeating the inner wisdom of your body and why caring physicians are becoming reluctant to prescribe these drugs. You will learn, step by step, about an alternative—not a pill, but a six-second skill called QR.

QR The Quieting Reflex

1. The Problem: Stress

Though she was an extremely talented pianist, 28-year-old Janet had never performed in public because she was too shy. As she dwelled on the conflict between her ambition for a musical career and her inability to play in front of audiences, Janet developed an increasing fear of going out in public at all, a condition that psychiatrists call *agoraphobia*. If she was away from home and sensed any crowding by other people, she began to breathe too hard or hyperventilate, she broke out in a cold sweat, became nauseated and found herself unable to move. Frequently she had to be escorted by the police back to the safety of her apartment, and many times they took her to a hospital emergency room. In time, by consulting twelve different doctors, Janet obtained multiple prescriptions for Valium, a minor tranquilizer, and built up to a habit of 400 milligrams a day—*ten times* the dose authorized by the Federal

Food and Drug Administration. But her habit rendered Janet almost incapable of playing the piano. She couldn't think clearly or coordinate her muscles well, and she was so sluggish and depressed that she was in danger of becoming suicidal.

Paul, a single, 44-year-old lawyer with a large criminal trial practice, approached his career and his social life with equal intensity. When he underwent his annual physical checkup, his doctor detected high blood pressure, a condition that, left untreated, can lead to heart attack or stroke. The medication that Paul's doctor prescribed brought his blood pressure under control, but it also rendered Paul sexually impotent.

Marion, a 38-year-old housewife, was a superachiever who placed extremely high demands on herself. She belonged to many women's clubs, was supportive of her husband in his career, and tried to be all things to her three children. But for twenty years, her life had been disrupted by excruciating migraine headaches that struck on the average of twice a month and persisted for about twenty-four hours. Marion's migraines had ruined her sexual relationship with her husband and had almost destroyed her family life. She and her husband had seen a family therapist but were nonetheless considering divorce.

Bernice, a 54-year-old housewife, doted on her grandchildren, who lived a continent away. But she rarely saw them. For twenty years, Bernice's entire way of life had been restricted by the fact that she experienced a need to go to the bathroom some fifteen to twenty times a day. She was afraid to travel by plane for fear that a lavatory wouldn't be available at all times. Bernice had consulted many medical specialists and tried many medications, but with little success. One doctor had suggested that the only answer was for her to start wearing diapers.

Ninety-Five Million Sufferers

Though the problems suffered by Janet, Paul, Marion and Bernice seem extremely different from one another, all their conditions are often caused or aggravated by exposure to the constant tension and stress of modern life. They are but four of an estimated 95 million people in this country who suffer from tension-related physical or psychological ailments. After the first years of childhood, people of any age or race and of either sex can fall prey to a wide variety of difficulties that can be traced in whole or in part to chronic stress.

Janet, Paul, Marion and Bernice are my own patients, and they all found the answer to their stress problems in a new technique called the Quieting Reflex, or QR. I originally developed QR as a result of my own tension-headache problem. As both doctor and patient, I learned that existing techniques were not effective long-term solutions to health problems brought on by tension and stress.

The role of stress in producing disease is not something I learned about in medical school. As soon as I got out of the hospital setting in which I was trained and began treating outpatients, however, the negative impact of stress on people's health began to become clear to me. Not only did it seem that chronic stress was causing many common health problems, but stress often caused people to panic and overreact to problems like pain, which only made their pain worse. In recent years, physicians have become increasingly aware of the role of stress in producing illness. Because they are not prepared to deal with stress problems, doctors often don't like to talk about the role of stress in producing illness, but most physicians now recognize that stress causes or accelerates between 70 and 90 percent of all medical complaints.

Muscle-tension headache and migraine headache, both of which are known to be stress related, together account for one-fifth of all complaints seen by doctors in general medical practice. Nervous stomach and bowel problems, which afflict between 15 and 20 percent of the population, are also stress related. So is chronic low back pain, the leading cause of work disability in America. And these are but a few of a broad spectrum of ailments that are now understood to be stress related. Even increased susceptibility to heart disease and cancer—our nation's two most devastating diseases—has in recent years been linked to exposure to chronic stress.

A "Type A" Society

The major reason that tension-related illnesses are so widespread is that we live in a society that both generates and rewards aggressive, competitive and achievement-oriented behavior. In 1974, two California cardiologists, Dr. Meyer Friedman and Dr. Ray H. Rosenman, published a book, *Type A Behavior and Your Heart*, in which they dubbed this driving personality "Type A" and reported that Type A people suffer significantly more heart attacks than other people. Their description of an individual preoccupied with work and achievement was so easily recognized by Americans that the term Type A quickly passed into popular language.

Despite Friedman and Rosenman's warnings about the health risks of being Type A, our society equates Type A behavior with success. We are achievement-oriented people, and we push our children toward excellence from their earliest years. I fit the Type A pattern myself, and if someone tried to teach me how to be Type B in order to have a healthy body, I would refuse. Aside from the negative health impact, I think being Type A represents a positive condition, the desirable state of the human brain and a state that most people are loath to give up. As I see it, when we consider the problem of stress-related illness, the major issue is how we can maintain the positive, high-performance traits of the Type A personality without devastating our physical health.

Early Alarms of Stress

At the heart of our stress-related difficulties is an ancient physiological mechanism that scientists call the "fight-or-flight"
response.

A day in the life of our primitive ancestors was often concerned with basic survival, pitting them against the wilderness
and its inhabitants. When these people came upon a dangerous
animal or enemy, their alternatives for action were clear: run
away or stand and fight. In the presence of danger or fear, their
bodies responded automatically to a signaling system within
the brain that altered their physical readiness—adrenaline surged
into their bloodstreams; they braced their muscles and clenched
their jaws, and their breathing and heart rates quickened. All
of these physical changes prepared them to run for safety or,
if necessary, to stand and fight. This reaction is known as the
"fight-or-flight" response, or the emergency response.

Our remarkable technological accomplishments notwith-
standing, modern human beings still occupy cavemen bodies.
Scientists generally agree that humans have not evolved mentally or physically in any significant way since prehistoric times.
The automatic emergency response is still present in all of us,
and it gives us the extra strength needed to fight or run to safety
when we're faced with real danger. This arousal mechanism
can be compared to the passing gear in a car, a wonderful
safety feature. When we get into a tight spot, we can push the
accelerator to the floor and zoom out of trouble.

Though modern man is physically much the same as his
ancestors, the perils he faces are not, and generally they are
not resolved by evoking the primitive fight-or-flight response.
As our society has grown in complexity, so has the environment
in which we live. The pressures we face have become increasingly mental, rather than physical. Take, for example, the problems of meeting our basic life-sustaining needs—securing food,
clothing and shelter. When we are hungry we buy food, rather
than face physical peril to secure it. We purchase clothing; we

don't have to kill and skin wild animals. And when we need shelter we enter a building; we don't have to do battle with an enemy for the nearest cave. Primitive man's life-sustaining activities involved physical threat and physical readiness, and appropriately called upon the emergency response. For modern humans, however, meeting these fundamental needs more often calls for complex mental activity.

Language, which can be manifested internally as fantasy, is also a crucial factor in the altered nature of human stress. Just by virtue of what we say, hear or think we generate inner tension and stress, and in so doing, we can arouse our bodies with the emergency response. If, for example, you are at home on a weekend and begin to think of your boss walking in on Monday and creating some sort of office crisis your body may physically react now to the stress you anticipate facing on Monday. In modern times, human beings have increasingly begun to exhibit the fight-or-flight response inappropriately with regard to time, place, or person.

Red, Pink or White Emergency Alerts

The emergency response is a hereditary protective mechanism. When it arises in reaction to a real physical threat to the body the situation can be thought of as a "red alert." The emergency response may be useful if you are faced with a catastrophic illness, if you are involved in an automobile accident, if you're coming face to face with Muhammad Ali in the boxing ring or if you otherwise have to defend yourself against physical aggression. Today, however, people are also subject to what I call "pink alerts" and "white alerts." In a pink alert, the emergency response is produced by merely thinking or worrying about a threat—the boss's morning rampage, money problems, or the likelihood that you may not be promoted at work. In a white alert, the emergency response arises from an unconscious, hidden or psychological source. A phobia, or unwarranted fear, is one example. Often a white alert involves a sense of lost security that has its roots in childhood experiences. If your boss is linked in your unconscious with an extremely punitive, demanding parental figure, for example, your interactions with him or her may produce behaviors you exhibited as a child. If, as inflation takes its toll, you feel that your retirement plans are giving way to an uncertain future, you may reexperience unconscious fears from your early years.

We simply cannot expect a purely physical response to cope adequately with most of the stress problems of our society. They're primarily mental problems, rather than body problems—saber-toothed cats are extinct. The red-alert condition is seldom needed, and neither the pink nor white alert is a useful protective mechanism.

There are still some situations in which the red alert, or emergency response, is appropriate. Watch athletes psych themselves before competition: a dominant element in their preparation is evoking a state of physical readiness, and we all have read of amazing feats of strength accomplished by people under the threat of physical harm, as in the case of fire. A soldier facing attack from an enemy and a policeman approaching a criminal are both in need of the emergency-response state. But most of us experience all of the physical changes of the emergency response in the face of everyday annoyances—when we're stuck in traffic behind someone who's straddling two lanes and driving 20 miles under the speed limit, or when we're hard at work and the ringing phone keeps interrupting—as well as when we're confronted by more serious mental challenges.

In today's rapidly moving, high-pressure world, we all are constantly bombarded with stressful situations. Ironically, when the fight-or-flight response is produced by stress that involves a mental challenge, it can reduce the very alertness needed to solve the problem. Can you think of a time when your boss suddenly called on you to answer a question and you "blocked" on it even though you knew the answer? Actual body measurements made in laboratories during similar situations indicate that most of us have a quick panic reaction, lasting six to ten seconds, that actually reduces our ability to perform. Anxiety can debilitate the way we function in many areas of our lives, including our careers. Actors need to be *somewhat* keyed up in order to give a good performance, but if they become overly tense, their bodies or voices may shake or they may forget their lines. The rest of us usually don't have an audience of hundreds: still anxiety can undermine us, too, in our daily lives.

Stress-Related Illnesses

But even more important, the strain that constant stress imposes on body and mind can actually produce illness.

If you drove a car in passing gear all the time, it would soon wear out. That is not an effective way to use an automobile, and it's not an effective way to use a body. But stressed people learn to overuse the passing gear so much that eventually they just don't know how to shift out of it. One of my own patients, Mike, an insurance agent with an aggressive, outgoing personality, developed both ulcers and high blood pressure. As a leading salesperson, Mike consistently won the all-expenses-paid vacations that his company offered as incentives. But Mike felt so uneasy when relieved of the tension that normally surrounded his selling activities that he came home only two days after the beginning of his first such vacation. After that, he always found convenient excuses for passing up vacation trips. People like Mike become so totally accustomed to a certain level of stress, and to the physical discomforts that accompany it, that they come to regard their condition as normal.

Doctors estimate that between 50 and 70 percent of all medical complaints are directly related to chronic inappropriate activation of the fight-or-flight response in the face of the stresses of daily life. These ailments include such cardiovascular difficulties as high blood pressure and migraine headaches; muscular disturbances including tension headache and backache; hormonal disturbances resulting in thyroid problems, obesity and skin problems; hyperventilation; various difficulties related to an irritable stomach or bowel condition; and asthma. When chronic activation of the emergency response persists over a period of several months, a number of additional conditions, accounting for perhaps 20 to 30 percent of medical complaints, may develop. These problems include reduced resistance to such infections as flus and colds, ulcers, kidney damage, increased incidence of heart attack and stroke, and increased susceptibility to cancer. Chronic stress is also a factor in a variety of nervous or psychological disturbances, including neurotic behaviors such as anxieties, phobias and obsessions; poor work performance; absenteeism; unexplained violence; use of drugs and alcohol; increased accidents; insomnia; creative blocks; depression and psychoses.

How Modern Medicine Misses the Mark

Traditional medicine which emphasizes surgery and medications is not effective in dealing with many stress-related diseases. The typical experience of someone suffering from tension headache, probably the most frequent of all medical complaints, illustrates its inadequacy.

Tension headache is produced by a spasm, or excessive contraction, of the muscles covering the skull, surrounding the joints of the jaw and sometimes in the neck, and is triggered by chronic activation of the emergency response, which entails bracing muscles and clenching the jaw. The pain is akin to a charley horse in a leg muscle, but it seems to come from within the head. Tension headaches are often chronic and debilitating, and frequently sufferers fear that they have some sort of brain tumor.

People suffering from such stress-related disorders are excessive users of the traditional health-care system. It is not unusual for a person with a twenty-year history of tension headaches to have sought medical evaluation in several major medical centers in the country every year. Often the patient is seeking reassurance that he or she does not have cancer. The cost of this pattern of repeated quests for help or reassurance is staggering, and it's a cost that can be measured not only in terms of misallocation of the resources of our expensive medical-care system, but in terms of the personal suffering and arrested personal growth of someone whose life is focused on his pain. People with pain problems often put incredible time and effort into seeing physicians and getting prescriptions filled, in consequence missing work and disrupting their social and family life. Often their pain comes to dominate most of their thinking moments. They worry and talk about it continually, and often, as a consequence, ruin their relationships with their families or coworkers.

One patient of mine, Adele, worried so much about the possibility that her headache pain might be caused by cancer that she sought out an average of three new doctors a week. Her handbag was filled with bottles of pills, and she talked so constantly about her headaches that her friends, family and fellow workers all began to avoid her. Adele was sure her death was imminent and she burdened her family with a tremendous load of guilt that totally restricted their social and home activities. Adele's problems consumed not only her own life, but the lives of those who came in contact with her.

Most physicians recognize that once a serious organic problem such as cancer has been ruled out, conscious or unconscious mental stress or anxiety is the most likely basis for the symptom of head pain. Initially, doctors simply reassure the patient that he doesn't have cancer and that tests have not detected any abnormalities. This reassurance may suffice for a time, but eventually as the symptom persists the patient experiences a nagging fear that the doctor didn't run the right test, or that the doctor received the wrong test results, or the patient believes that some new discovery or diagnostic technique will at last reveal the source of the problem. After the CAT scan procedure for detecting brain masses was introduced several years ago, headache patients all over the country made appointments at facilities with CAT scanners, hopefully seeking the final resolution of their headache problems; most scans produced negative results.

One of the problems with the reassurance physicians give patients is that many doctors are not comfortable or skilled in playing a reassuring role. Modern medical schools are primarily concerned with equipping doctors with the knowledge and skills of their trade, the repair of the malfunctioning body. Students have to learn so much about the physical and technological aspects of medicine that there is little time for less concrete subjects, such as the *art* of medicine. Prior to the advent of modern surgical techniques and drugs, however, that art was the primary skill of the physician. He cured by being present and by being reassuring, which helped to mobilize the patient's own resources.

Today, because we do have scientifically based skills, doctors have a tendency to treat patients almost as objects. They give an injection or perform surgery, but spend very little time helping to reduce the patient's worries about his health. Medical schools give only lip service to the art of medicine, although they have begun to recognize its importance again as family practitioners return to popularity. This appreciation of the art of medicine will probably become stronger as we learn more about the scientific basis of stress physiology. Our understanding of the art of medicine itself will become more scientific, and medical schools will then find it more acceptable as part of their programs.

In current medical practice, the physician plays an active role and the patient plays a passive role. When you become a patient, your part in the healing process is usually minimal. Normally all the doctor asks is that you follow his or her treatment plan, which may mean taking medication on schedule or showing up for specialized tests. A coworker who had spent some time in the hospital recently described to me the effect of this doctor-patient relationship. "You have almost no say in what is going on and you somehow become less than a whole person," she told me. "You're at the mercy of hospital personnel—doctors, nurses, technicians, even the cleaning staff—twenty-four hours a day. You eat on schedule and take medications on schedule, not always to your own maximum benefit. You are always being acted upon." The sense of powerlessness that afflicts many patients can be demoralizing and even demeaning, yet most doctors and patients have come to accept this pattern as appropriate.

Suspicion of Psychological Solutions

Currently, many physicians would like to refer stress-symptom patients to a psychologist or psychiatrist who is more trained than they in giving reassurance and helping people understand stress mechanisms. They've learned, however, that most patients experiencing stress-related pain reject such referrals. These patients believe the problem is not in their minds but in their bodies, for their pain is very real. When referred to a psychiatrist, the typical tension-headache patient privately thinks, "Doctor, you're the one who's got something wrong with his head!"

A Seemingly Simple Solution

Currently, the most "acceptable" alternative for the physician treating a patient with a stress-related disorder is to prescribe a minor tranquilizer such as Valium, Serax, Tranxene or Librium—all contain chemicals that are highly effective in dampening the initial phases of the emergency response. This approach is often reinforced by patients, who have come to expect pills from doctors and believe that pills will make them well. A significant problem with this approach is that people often develop a psychological dependency on tranquilizers that creates a vicious circle: Each time you dampen the stress pathway by taking a minor tranquilizer, you are able to take on more stressful activities, until you reach the breaking point again. Then you start increasing your dosage. Minor tranquilizers are the most commonly prescribed class of drugs, with approximately 10 million Americans taking 500 billion pills each year. While brief use of these drugs during short periods of acute crisis is highly effective and appropriate, they should not be prescribed for the routine stresses and strains of living.

If you are currently taking a minor tranquilizer, or if your physician is considering prescribing one for you, you have perhaps been reassured by reports in the popular press suggesting that no physical addiction develops from these medications as long as dosages do not exceed federally approved limits. Scientists are divided on this issue, but it is clear that even when doses remain within these limits, a strong psychological dependency does develop. In addition, many people soon escalate their dosage beyond what their doctors have prescribed. Hospitals are admitting an increasing number of people who have reached a dosage requirement of up to ten times that

recommended for some of the minor tranquilizers, and withdrawal has frequently proved more difficult than for alcohol,
heroin or morphine.

When people take such high doses of tranquilizers, their
mental alertness becomes so suppressed that they find themselves unable to function at home, at work or in social situations. Barbara Gordon's *I'm Dancing as Fast as I Can*, a
harrowing account of one woman's ordeal with tranquilizer
dependency, is must reading for anyone who is beginning to
sense a need for increased levels of tranquilizers.

In 1979, a Senate committee chaired by Senator Edward
Kennedy got the pharmaceutical companies that produce minor
tranquilizers to agree to label them as inappropriate for long-
term use in dealing with everyday problems. Physicians are
becoming more hesitant to prescribe these drugs for the strains
of ordinary living, but until now, no satisfactory alternative
has been available.

The Behavioral Revolution

A major source of proposed alternatives in recent years has
been the relatively new field of behavioral medicine—sometimes called health psychology—which has developed as a
result of a growing recognition of the inadequacy of traditional
medical approaches to many chronic health problems.

In modern times, the medical profession has undergone two
major revolutions. The first was the advent of anesthesia and
antisepsis, which permitted dependable surgery. The second
was the development of effective chemotherapies—first anti-
biotics, and then other medications. But one day we are going
to reach the limits of what doctors can do for us technically.
The new behavioral medicine, concerned with what people can
do for themselves, is going to represent the medical profession's
third revolution.

Practitioners of behavioral medicine recognize that the mind
has communication with every cell in the body and can influence the body toward health or disease. That continual tension
and stress are reflected in an increased incidence of a whole

spectrum of mental and physical ills is itself an illustration of this fact. The other side of this situation, however, is that human beings possess inherent capabilities to prevent illness in themselves and to restore health when illness occurs. Research has proved that the mind can be trained to play an important part in preventing disease and in overcoming it when it occurs. The popular book *Anatomy of an Illness*, in which author Norman Cousins recounts how he overcame a serious illness with an unorthodox approach that included spending many hours watching funny movies and reading humorous literature, is a striking account of how mental attitude can affect health.

Recent years have seen the popularization of a variety of "self-regulation" techniques aimed at teaching people to acquire control of disturbed inner body functions in order to normalize them and restore health. These techniques include Transcendental Meditation, or TM; the Relaxation Response (a TM derivative); and biofeedback. Controlled studies have shown that these and similar methods are remarkably effective in enabling people to reverse such health problems as high blood pressure and migraine headache. These initially impressive techniques have been flawed, however, primarily by what scientists call "poor transfer of training" and "low compliance over the long term." That is to say, despite the striking health benefits that many people derive from learning these techniques, a high percentage have difficulty carrying their new self-regulation skills out of the practice situation and into everyday life; and many stop practicing within a few months of their initial training. Even after finding relief from chronic low back pain, for example, a patient may begin to find excuses for giving up the technique that has helped, saying, "I just can't find time to practice," or "My children are always interrupting me." Often these people have a belief structure that says, "Let the doctor or the pills fix me." They are unwilling to accept the idea that they can help themselves, and usually this belief structure is reinforced by the fact that their employers or health insurance companies compensate them for seeking medical solutions.

A Simple, Automatic Technique

In this book, you will read about a new self-regulation skill, the Quieting Reflex, that solves the problems of poor transfer of training and low compliance. The Quieting Reflex, or QR, is a simple, six-second technique that prevents the fight-or-flight response from being activated except when it is appropriate and thus can prevent or reverse illnesses brought on by continual inappropriate activation of the emergency response. QR differs from earlier self-regulation techniques in two highly significant ways. First, QR is compatible with the demands of our high-pressure society and does not require dropping out or slowing down in order to preserve your health. QR permits you to function with an achievement-oriented Type A personality without suffering negative physical consequences—to maintain your Type A mind in a Type B body. Second, after an initial learning period, QR becomes *automatic*—whenever your body is about to undergo the emergency response inappropriately, the QR is activated at a subconscious level. Once you've achieved the automatic QR, no further practice is necessary. QR is with you for life. In fact, ongoing research suggests that, like the emergency response, the Quieting Reflex is an inborn capacity, but that the continual stress of modern life overwhelms this capacity in many people. Training in QR, then, represents a way to reclaim this natural mechanism for preventing stress-related disease.

As succeeding chapters describe, I originally developed the QR technique as a result of my search for a solution to my own tension-headache problem. Since that time, some 1200 people have learned the QR technique under my supervision. Among them are Janet, Paul, Marion and Bernice—the four patients described in the opening pages. QR enabled each of them to overcome their stress problems without medication. Today, approximately 4000 clinicians in this country and abroad are using the QR technique with their own patients, and their experience has confirmed that it is effective in dealing with such varied health problems as migraine headache, low back pain, irritable stomach and bowel, high blood pressure, and many kinds of anxieties.

This book contains all the materials and instructions you need to learn the Quieting Reflex. Learning QR will require only a small investment of your time. Eight initial training sessions, each lasting less than half an hour, will familiarize you with the sensations of the Quieting Reflex. Each evening, you will take a few moments to fill out the QR Diary Scan, pages 101—102, on which you will chart the level of stress that you experienced that day, then practice the QR Bedtime Daily Review Exercise (see page 153) as you lie in bed ready to fall asleep. And until you achieve automaticity—a period of four to six months for most adults—you will consciously practice the six-second QR technique throughout the day whenever you encounter stress or tension. With the information on these pages, you can take control of the impact of stress on your health and help yourself avoid the myriad of stress-related illnesses for the rest of your life.

2. My Search for an Answer to Stress

As a physician and a psychiatrist, I have been interested in research into the relationship between stress and disease for many years. But about a decade ago this interest took on more personal significance when stress began to take its toll on my own well-being.

My life at that time seemed to be filled with annoyances, worries, time pressures and repeated crises at home or work, and these stresses grew worse every day. I began to dread taking vacations, knowing that I'd be faced with a pile of problems, big and small, when I returned. When I did take time off, even if just for a nap, my mind was not at rest. I felt I couldn't *really* take time off, for there was just too much to be done.

Inevitably, my body rebelled. I developed excruciating tension headaches that appeared regularly at three o'clock every afternoon, no matter how hard I tried to slow my pace. My head pains were so terrible that I did indeed become convinced that I had a brain tumor. Then instead of slowing down I panicked. Over the next several years, I consulted many doctors. Although I was a physician myself, I became a doctor shopper because none of the doctors I consulted could find anything organically wrong with me. My continuing hope was that the next doctor would miraculously detect and cure my problem.

Most of the doctors I saw suggested that the problem was all in my mind, and together they prescribed a closetful of minor tranquilizers and painkillers that never helped for more than a day or two. In time it dawned on me that in addition to offering patch-up medication and assuring me that I didn't have cancer, all of these doctors issued one piece of simple advice. "Stop worrying," they told me. "Just relax."

I realized then that I didn't know *how* to "stop worrying" and "just relax," even though I repeated the same advice to many of my own patients every day. My medical and surgical training and my subsequent specialty training in psychiatry and neurology had prepared me to be a caring and scientific physician but they hadn't taught me anything about how to relax or how to help others do so.

The Visible Impact of Stress

About this time, I had lunch with a senior colleague whose wisdom I deeply respected. She was easily as busy as I, and I asked what advice on relaxation she gave in counseling her patients, how she dealt with the stresses in her own life. She didn't answer directly. "Chuck," she said, "why don't you spend some time tonight looking through your family photo album at pictures of you taken over the last ten years? Try to observe yourself objectively, as though the pictures were of another person. Look for changes in your facial expression, your body posture, and the way you come across to others."

That evening, I sat down with my 8-year-old son, Chuckie, to look at family albums covering the years since 1960. It was like looking at time-lapse photography. As we moved from one year to the next, Chuck commented that he could see I was getting older because I had slowly put on weight. I was astounded, however, at the progressive changes in my facial expression, which seemed to grow more grim and determined with passing time. My smile had changed over the years, becoming increasingly plastic and artificial. My eyes had dulled. My posture, natural and relaxed when I was younger, had become rigid and stiff, especially in the way I carried my shoulders and arms. The gradual but undeniable change in my appearance showed that I had adjusted bodily to increasing stress and tension without being aware of it. And most of these pictures had been taken when I was having fun with my family! Apparently my body remained tense even when I thought I was happy and relaxed.

Seeing these changes in the way I carried myself suggested that studying "body awareness" might provide the answer to my questions about how to relax. So I read books and took a course in a technique designed to eliminate faulty muscle tension by developing effortless movement. When I was in class working with my teacher, I did feel noticeably better. Unfortunately, when I was on my own, I found myself concentrating so much on my smile and posture that my tension actually seemed to intensify.

A New Path—Meditation

My next course of action was suggested to me by Bernard C. Glueck, M.D., a colleague at the behavioral medicine clinic where I was working. Bernard has been my mentor and teacher since 1959 when I entered graduate school at the University of Minnesota where he was head of the department of psychiatry. More recently, he had become intrigued with meditation and was studying its effectiveness. He told me that for hundreds of years British physicians had reported that yogis in India could self-regulate their body functions to a remarkable degree. They could control their respiration, remaining in airtight enclosures long beyond the time untrained human beings could endure, and they could control their heart rates and the flow of blood from wounds. Yoga involved asceticism, celibacy and other rigors, and frequently a thirty-year training period, but a less demanding variety of meditation, called "Transcendental Meditation," also offered the possibility of self-regulation of body functions—though to a less dramatic degree—and was better suited to Westerners. Perhaps TM would enable me to gain control of the muscle tension that produced my excruciating headaches.

TM had been introduced to the Western world in the 1960s by the Indian Maharishi Mahesh Yogi, and received great notoriety when it was adopted by a number of celebrities, including the Beatles, who were then at the height of their career. TM is simple, requiring four to six hours of verbal instruction. It is entirely mental, requiring no physical exercise or special diet. The technique consists of sitting passively, with eyes closed, for about twenty minutes twice a day, thinking to oneself a Sanskrit word, or *mantra*, that is given to the meditator by the instructor.

When I began looking into TM, a growing collection of experimental data showed that experienced meditators could produce relatively specific, unique and consistent changes in their bodies that were incompatible with the body's normal response to stress. They could, for example, prevent the release of the stress hormone adrenaline, thus maintaining constant levels of breathing, heart rate and sweating under stressful conditions that would provoke accelerated levels of all three in untrained individuals. This ability to control the body's response to stress meant meditators could prevent or relieve a variety of disorders that have been linked to chronic stress.

I went through the TM training program and began to practice enthusiastically twice a day, before breakfast and dinner. At first I sensed some relief from my tension problem. But after several weeks I began to experience distressing muscle twitches during meditation. The instructors assured me that this was a normal occurrence—they called it "unstressing"—but I became alarmed when I began to develop new tension headaches immediately after meditation. (I didn't know it then, but some studies have shown that meditation makes headaches worse, a result of what psychiatrists call the "after-the-battle phenomenon"—as the meditator relaxes and lowers his usual defenses, tension that was previously beneath the level of awareness is released, producing a worsening of symptoms.)

Consciously or unconsciously, I began to find excuses not to meditate, and three months after beginning, I had stopped entirely. Later I would learn that most meditators who do not become instructors themselves stop meditating within a relatively short time, either because they lose contact with the support system of an instructor and group, or because the need for twice-daily meditation sessions is incompatible with their life-styles.

Body Conversations

Ironically, after months of searching, I achieved the first breakthrough in my headache problem with a technique I worked with every day. Using biofeedback to lower muscle tension gave me the first really significant relief from my headaches. Looking back, I can't believe I was so slow to try it. In my work at the clinic, as part of a research study, I was training people to use biofeedback equipment to relieve their stress-related illnesses. Biofeedback technique had been developed only a few years before, in the late 1960s, and was just being popularized as a superior way to show people that they could control much of what goes on in their bodies and thus avoid or relieve many ailments. Somehow, though, I just didn't believe that biofeedback could be as miraculous as it was claimed to be. I had to see sixty headache patients go through biofeedback training and experience remarkable improvement before my skepticism died and I decided I'd better get into it myself.

The term "feedback," borrowed from engineering, refers to the "feeding back" of information to the mechanism producing it. Biofeedback involves feedback from various body systems to the brain. Some body systems have extensive feedback reporting to the conscious brain, others do not. We are aware of the information gathered by our five senses, for example, and we are aware of the positions of our legs and arms as they are moved through space by our skeletal muscles because we have feedback from these systems. As part of a standard neurological examination, the patient is asked to close his eyes and touch his left index finger to the tip of his nose. Most people perform this exercise with ease, using extensive feedback as to the position of finger and nose and effectively carrying out differential calculus in three dimensions. This apparently simple feat, which most of us take for granted, could not be carried out by the world's fastest computer with the speed that it is accomplished by the human brain.

By contrast, we are relatively unaware of the workings of the "involuntary" inner machinery of our bodies that controls our blood pressure or gastrointestinal activity, the functioning of our hearts, or the regulation of smooth muscles in our arteries. And fortunately so. If we had to consciously concern ourselves with squirting a little acid into our stomachs as part of the digestive process, or with opening and closing each of the four heart valves to maintain blood flow through the body, or with increasing our blood pressure to avoid fainting when we stand up, we would have no time left for the unique intellectual and other functions that characterize the richness of human existence.

Information on the conscious level from our inner body systems remains meager unless one of them malfunctions. Then the major feedback signal is the relatively crude sensation of pain, and even this signal can be misleading, for sometimes pain is "referred," or felt in an area away from the actual site of the problem.

The principle of biofeedback is that an "involuntary" inner body function can be brought under conscious control by mechanically monitoring it and converting it to an external signal that can be observed by the conscious mind. An electrical, temperature or pressure sensor is used, depending on the condition under treatment and the body system that needs to be monitored. The feedback signal is either a sound or a visual display. In a typical application, sensors that register the temperature of the skin's surface are attached to a subject's fingertips. The sensors are connected to a feedback machine that emits an observable signal, such as a sound that rises in pitch when the subject's skin temperature rises and falls when the skin temperature drops. Provided with this new "feedback," the subject can learn relatively quickly to control the flow of blood to his fingers so that he can raise or lower his skin temperature at will. Biofeedback makes the normally involuntary function available to the conscious brain so that it can use its capacity for learning to acquire voluntary control. (The first person to demonstrate the practicability of self-regulation of body machinery with biofeedback was Neal Miller, Ph.D., professor of psychobiology at Rockefeller University in New York City. His initial work, involving experiments with laboratory rats, was conducted at Yale University in the late 1950s.)

Ironically, the person using biofeedback cannot learn to raise his skin temperature by concertedly *trying* to increase the blood flow to his fingers. Indeed, when he first *tries* to raise his skin temperature, he almost invariably achieves the opposite effect. In order to succeed, he needs to achieve a state of "passive volition," telling his body to do something and then letting it happen. To accomplish this, the biofeedback "hardware"—the instrument—is used in conjunction with a "software" program—a set of instructions and coaching that helps the person achieve quieting, which is accomplished by a relaxation of constricted blood vessels. (These terms are borrowed from the computer field, where "hardware" refers to a computer, and "software" to the programming or instructions used to operate it.) The biofeedback software approaches quieting in an indirect way, and even when people have learned to control a function like blood flow through biofeedback, they generally find it difficult to describe how they do it.

Characteristically, when people develop some degree of proficiency in following the software instructions, they begin to experience sensations of flowing heaviness and flowing warmth in their bodies. After an initial learning period, the objective is to be able to produce these same sensations and maintain control of inner body function without relying on the biofeedback device.

Monitoring Forehead Tension

As already described, my problem, tension headache, is produced by a spasm of muscles covering the skull. This is one manifestation of excess stress affecting the voluntary, or skeletal muscles—the muscles used to move the arms, legs and other parts of the skeleton, the eyes and the vocal cords.

While movement of the skeletal muscles is normally under voluntary control, the levels of basic tension in them are maintained by the *gamma efferent* system, which is under unconscious control. The gamma efferent system consists of small information-carrying loops around every muscle fiber in your body that make sure your muscles are never slack. If you're carrying out a series of complicated coordinated movements, as in playing tennis or running, your brain has to coordinate millions of neural impulses and muscle fibers. If there were slackness in any one of the hundreds of muscles involved in such an activity, your brain would get hopelessly muddled trying to calculate the time involved in taking up the slack and actually starting to move your body. The gamma efferent system, therefore, makes sure that your muscles are never slack. Because of unconscious mental factors or the stress and strain of life, however, people learn to *overset* the gamma efferent system so the muscles are like taut strings, *too* ready to go into action. This burns up so much excess energy that it can cause fatigue, and it can also produce or worsen tension-headache and backache problems.

Since I needed to gain control of the muscles covering my skull, during my biofeedback training I was hooked up to a device called an electromyograph, or EMG machine, which detects muscle tension below the level of normal awareness. Three sensors attached to my forehead picked up electrical signals given off by the muscles located there. The feedback signal produced by the EMG apparatus was the amplified sound of the muscle activity detected by the sensors. It sounded like static and grew in intensity when the muscle tension increased.

This "on-line," or immediate, reporting of muscle activity provided me with essential information about my body's functioning to which I had never before been privy. Over time, my hookup to the biofeedback device enabled me to privately and systematically recognize the mental images and processes that increased or decreased tension levels in my body. When I was first attached to the EMG instrument, I was amazed that virtually every thought I had prompted a loud crackling of the feedback signal. It didn't surprise me that my muscles tensed when I was thinking about something that had made me angry the day before. But my muscles also reacted strongly to less upsetting thoughts, when I felt I was calm, cool and collected; the very act of thinking seemed to set them off. I could hardly believe that so much muscle activity was going on without my awareness. After about eight weekly training sessions, however, I learned to control my muscles so they didn't respond excessively to my every thought. Although I continued to suffer occasional "breakthrough" headaches, I had almost conquered my headache problem.

A Powerful But Flawed Technique

Now I was convinced that biofeedback was a remarkable self-mastery technique for correcting malfunctioning body machinery. Like tension headache, migraine headache had also proven very amenable to control through biofeedback, and together these two problems account for about *one-fifth* of all complaints coming into general medical practice! The effectiveness of biofeedback had also been demonstrated for other conditions, including Raynaud's disease (a circulatory disorder of which constricted blood vessels, resulting in cold and blanched fingers or toes, are a symptom), some forms of neurologic injury, and general stress. And because of its use of instrumentation and its dramatic capacity to reveal to a trainee the presence of unconscious tension states in different organ systems, biofeedback had greater appeal for Americans than some other self-regulation techniques, such as meditation.

While I recognized the logic and appeal of biofeedback,

however, I became concerned about problems with compliance—retaining the learning and continuing to practice. One can't carry a biofeedback machine around with him, and the technique is learned in a quiet setting, away from the stress of life. My colleagues and I saw a very significant improvement in patients only as long as we had active contact with them and encouraged them to practice for twenty minutes twice a day in a quiet room at home, as a substitute for the clinic. We used various techniques—having them put little stickers on their hands or watches, or set little parking-meter alarms to go off every half hour, or turn a ring backwards—to remind them frequently during the day to recall the feelings of heaviness and warmth that they'd experienced with biofeedback. But we found that everybody became accustomed to these reminders almost immediately and stopped practicing within two or three days.

I became very concerned that this powerful self-mastery technique might fall into disuse simply because the "transfer of training" outside the initial learning situation wasn't good unless we saw people endlessly in therapeutic reminder sessions. I recognized that my own "breakthrough" headaches were due to a failure to practice—a typical Type A, I found the daily sessions too time-consuming and inconvenient—and that I was becoming too dependent on review sessions with the biofeedback apparatus. In order to remain headache free, I had to go back to the machines about every two weeks. It seemed to me that the potential of biofeedback for preventive medicine would not be realized unless a self-reinforcing technique—a pleasurable technique that brought quick results—was incorporated into it to insure that the training was transferred outside the initial learning setting for long-term effectiveness.

3. The Answer: QR

In 1974, I set about developing a new set of instructions to be used with biofeedback training. The "software" we were using at the clinic at that time consisted of instruction in a variety of existing self-regulation techniques, and was read aloud to patients while they were hooked up to the biofeedback instruments. Because I had to repeat similar material to each person I saw, by the third hour in my day, my voice began to lose its spontaneity, and patients started to pick up on it. I decided that it would be better to tape the material, apologize for the seeming impersonality, and assure people that there'd be time at the beginning and end of each session for us to talk personally.

My primary objectives in preparing the audio-cassette program were to standardize the quality of instruction for each person and to synthesize exercises from the various self-regulation techniques in a systematic fashion, producing a software program more inclusive than any then in existence. But as I began, my attention focused on the larger issue of compliance; I wanted to develop a pleasant, results-producing technique that would be carried into the real world outside the training situation on a permanent basis.

After reviewing the basic psychological principles underlying the transfer of a newly learned skill from a training setting into the real world, I recognized that we needed a technique that was quick—as fast as "popping a pill"—and virtually automatic. (Compliance is not a problem with the minor tranquilizers—the ease and quickness with which one can take them are part of the reason they're so widely used.) I also decided that we needed a technique that people could use instantaneously, at the moment of stress, while they were carrying out alert mental activity. Dr. Meyer Friedman and Dr. Ray H. Rosenman had just published *Type A Behavior and Your Heart*, which describes how "Type A Behavior Pattern"—a complex of behavior traits including excess competitive drive, aggressiveness, impatience and a sense of time urgency—produced coronary disease tendencies. But I knew that my clinic patients wanted to maintain the positive qualities of Type A behavior, in the sense of being high achievers who face a lot of time pressures.

I adopted Friedman and Rosenman's concept of Type A and Type B behavior, but I amplified it by distinguishing between mental tension and body tension. Mental tension is the culprit when you find yourself lying in bed trying to sleep, with a body that feels physically tired but a mind that is restless and won't stop thinking or going over the day's events. Body tension is the problem when your mind is extremely fatigued from the day's activities, but your body is restless and you can't find a position in bed that will permit you to fall asleep.

Certainly mental and body tension are interrelated; Friedman and Rosenman's point was that Type A mental behavior eventually produces symptoms in the body. But differentiating between mental tension and body tension enabled me to set a new goal. I began to wonder if it might be possible to maintain a Type A mind in a Type B body.

I decided we needed a technique that would enable us to interrupt the stress mechanism early on, giving a person the choice of whether or not to activate the body with the fight-or-flight response. If we could interrupt the physical emergency response when it wasn't needed to deal with stress with a pleasurable countermeasure, we might achieve the desired compliance and also permit people to function on the job involving Type A mental activity without putting excessive stress on their bodies.

The Process of Shifting Into Passing Gear

The initial emergency response can be broken down roughly into five steps. Though the sequence varies from person to person, the first step is usually increased vigilance—paying attention to what is frightening or potentially harmful in the environment. Frequently, this step is felt in a flush reaction, wetness of the hands, or a tendency to perspire generally. Almost simultaneously, there is a perking of attention and a tensing of the muscles of the face, which becomes grim. About three seconds into the emergency response, there is a catching of the breath, or shallow, quick breathing like panting. Next the jaws clench. Finally, there is frequently a drop in the temperature of the hands and feet, which become cold and clammy. All these changes, which can be measured by laboratory instruments, take place within six seconds.

The Six-Second QR

After reviewing all this information, I formulated what I called the "six-second Quieting Response." The first step of the Quieting Response, like the first step of the emergency response, was an awareness of something frightening or annoying in the environment. But the succeeding steps—quick, conscious steps that could be carried out unobtrusively in the space of six seconds—comprised the precise counterpart of the physiology of the first six seconds of the emergency response. The two were diametrically opposed to one another and could not occur together.

I incorporated this six-second Quieting Response into my new instruction program, which consisted of eight cassettes to be used during the first eight sessions of biofeedback training for people suffering from stress-related disorders. The early sessions led the trainee through a variety of body-awareness and quieting procedures. The last cassette, intended to promote the practice and transfer of biofeedback training and the related feelings of flowing heaviness and warmth into the real world, concluded with the six-second Quieting Response.

As already mentioned, the first step of the Quieting Response, like the first step of the emergency response, is an awareness of something frightening or annoying in the environment. Patients were instructed to practice the six-second technique throughout the day whenever they encountered an annoyance, tension or anxiety—if they found themselves with too many appointments booked into their schedule, for example, or if they got caught in a snowstorm on the way to work. This instruction solved one of the basic problems with compliance in practicing. People might quickly begin to ignore stickers on their watches or pocket parking-meter alarms, but the one stimulus they couldn't ignore was something that got on their nerves or annoyed them.

By interrupting the emergency response, the Quieting Response created a six-second pause during which a person could decide whether or not to activate his body. If a physical emergency response was really called for, it could still occur. But the Quieting Response allowed a person to recognize that most worries or annoyances don't call for a "passing-gear" body. Many people find it extremely stressful to have to give somebody a negative decision—to have to inform someone they can't meet a deadline or fire someone, for example—but experiencing butterflies in the stomach and elevated blood pressure doesn't make the task any easier.

By practicing the Quieting Response myself, I at last gained permanent freedom from my headaches. The first patients that I trained in the Quieting Response were also excited with the results. At follow-ups after six months, one year and two years, the incidence of people remaining symptom free—and by their

own accounts with their whole lives changed for the better—
was much higher than we had ever heard of in terms of a
compliance figure.

Even more exciting was the discovery that after a period of
practice, the Quieting Response became automatic! One didn't
have to think about performing it; it simply happened spontaneously when stress was experienced, triggered by the catch
or alteration in breathing rhythm that is one of the steps of the
emergency response. I remember very clearly the first time it
happened to me. I was watching a TV movie with my son
Chuckie, and one scene involved a violent car crash. Normally,
I would have grabbed my chair and tensed up, just watching.
Instead, something in my brain seemed to say, "Why get uptight
about this?" and I felt the pleasant sensations of the Quieting
Response flow through my body.

A few weeks later, there was a meeting of the clinic staff,
several of whom had been practicing the Quieting Response.
We were discussing the progress of various patients, when one
nurse volunteered, "I've begun to have the QR happen to me
all the time, without thinking about it." I said that the same
thing had been happening to me. When several other staff
members chimed in about their own experiences, we suddenly
realized that the Quieting Response was becoming an inherent
part of our behavior.

We didn't tell our patients that the QR would become automatic, however. Instead, we waited to see if they would tell
us spontaneously that QRs were occurring without their conscious awareness of a cue. And about 95 percent of the people
did report automaticity at the follow-up visit scheduled six
months after the start of training. An example of a typical
patient report would be, "I sensed that good feeling of flowing
heaviness, warmth and mastery at the very second my boss put
me on the spot."

With practice, then, the voluntary Quieting Response became an involuntary Quieting *Reflex*. If the emergency response
is like a car's passing gear, then the Quieting Response, called
forth voluntarily when one encounters annoyances or tension,
was akin to a manual gearshift, and the Quieting Reflex could
be compared to an automatic gearshift, which operates without
conscious manipulation.

In fact, it now appears that the Quieting Reflex, like the emergency response, is inborn, but that the pressures of modern life often overwhelm our quieting capacity as we mature. The fact that children learn the six-second QR technique much more quickly than adults supports this theory. Indeed, stress is usually not a significant problem for children until they are subjected to the constraints and pressures of school.

Quieting is not the same as relaxation. A person can experience quieting even when he is active and sensing stress. With quieting, bodies of healthy people should quickly recover normal balance after their initial reaction to stress. Many of us have unconsciously taught our bodies to override our natural responses until constant tension, anxiety and tightness begin to seem normal to us. Training in QR helps us regain the capacity we had as young children to recover quickly from excessive stress. A number of professional colleagues, after hearing my talks, have become enthusiastic about the QR concept, but some have missed the point of being able to shift gears up *or* down as appropriate. They talk about QR—Quick Reflex, or QR—Quick Response. But quickly shifting down to "relax" is not always appropriate, as we shall see in chapter 6, when we examine in more detail my patient Marion's migraine-headache problem, which I presented briefly in chapter 1.

The Benefits of Biofeedback Without Instruments

I began describing the documented clinical successes of QR to professional audiences, and soon I realized that perhaps a third of those who heard me—and I wasn't presenting any of the training exercises included in this book—would approach me afterward and say, "While you were talking, I began to have the feelings in my body that you described." It dawned on me that *QR could be taught without the use of biofeedback instrumentation!*

After that, if a person to whom I explained the QR rationale and the basic steps leading to it seemed to grasp the idea and reported that he was able to experience the desired sensations of flowing heaviness and warmth, I asked him to complete the QR program without biofeedback. My colleagues and I found that simply by teaching people the experiential—that is, feeling and doing—exercises, we could produce in them precisely the same sensations that people experienced with biofeedback machines. Over the next few years, we established that well over 80 percent of the people who came to us could master the QR technique without using biofeedback equipment at all.

A Systematic Training Program

As presented in this book, QR training is composed of the daily use of a QR Diary Scan, pages 101—102, to heighten your awareness of the stresses in your life that trigger the emergency response; a series of experiential training exercises; a nightly QR Bedtime Review Exercise, page 153; and practice of the six-second technique at the very moment stressful events occur. The experiential training is divided into eight sessions, each requiring less than half an hour of your time, to be practiced at intervals of about one week. In each session, imagery and exercises are used to produce sensations of flowing heaviness and warmth like those experienced during biofeedback training. The sensations accompanying each of the components of the six-second technique are explored individually and at length, and are then combined into shorter exercises that lead to the six-second response and, finally, the six-second reflex.

Your very first QR will produce good physical sensations and a sense of positive stress control. Learning QR takes time, however, just as it takes time to learn to tie your shoes, type without looking at the keyboard, play tennis or drive a car. At first the steps have to be practiced consciously, but eventually they become automatic. The transition between the Quieting Response and the Quieting Reflex does not occur instantaneously or miraculously. It requires continuing practice each time you encounter an annoyance, over a period that averages between four and six months for most adults. This learning process is best represented as a learning curve, as illustrated in Figure 1. Once you have achieved automaticity, daily practice is no longer needed. The Quieting Reflex becomes a routine part of your life and occurs at the very moment of inappropriate stress.

Life-changing Impact

For me personally, after seven years, QR remains automatic virtually 100 percent of the time. Only on occasion do I have to "do" a conscious QR, usually in a situation where it's not

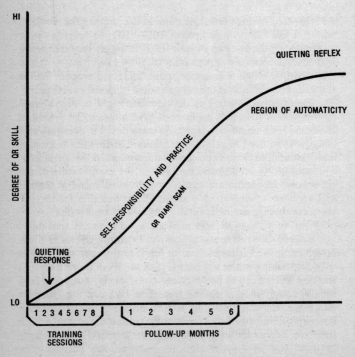

Figure 1

quite clear whether I really need to get "uptight." In providing permanent relief from the daily tension headaches that plagued me prior to 1973, QR has been a miracle. QR has also relieved other stress problems that used to trouble me, such as performance anxiety before public lectures, and insomnia. More profoundly, by releasing the grip of inappropriate stress on my health and well-being, QR has improved my whole outlook on life.

At the time of this writing, about 1200 people have gone through QR training under my supervision. In addition, some 4000 professionals working with large clinic populations in the United States and abroad are using the audio-cassette program available since 1976, bringing the number of people who have undergone QR training to an estimated 400,000. The material in this book has been distilled through my experience and the experiences of those 4000 other professionals.

In my work with patients, I have seen QR bring relief from a wide range of physical and psychological problems including migraine headache, irritable stomach and bowel, hypertension, and pain and depression related to cancer therapy, compulsive tendencies and various types of creative "blocks." For people with many of these problems, QR has provided an alternative to drugs that were either ineffective, produced unpleasant side effects, involved a risk of addiction or dependency, or simply relieved symptoms without getting at the basic cause behind them—chronic excessive activation of the emergency response. Like me, better than 80 percent of the people who have gone through the six-month QR program and experienced symptom relief say that QR has changed their whole attitude toward life.

To many, this last claim may seem like dramatic overstatement—unless one knows what it's like to live with a chronic, debilitating stress problem, as I did. A person who suffers chronic stress-related pain may find his whole life revolving around his problem. When he isn't actually experiencing pain, he's busy trying to avoid the circumstances that bring it on or pursuing medical and nonmedical ways to alleviate it. Finding relief from such pain can seem a true miracle.

Self-mastery and Self-responsibility

The life-changing impact of QR is also related to the realization
that one has greater control over what happens in one's body
than most of us appreciate. People with chronic health problems
often feel dependent on physicians and medication, and achieving self-mastery and self-responsibility with QR can indeed
change their outlook on life to an extent that cannot yet be
measured.

Among the hundreds of people to whom I have taught QR
is Judith, a psychologist in her fifties, who had breast cancer
that had begun to spread widely throughout her body. Immediately after undergoing a mastectomy, she was referred to me
for consultation about pain problems that she was expected to
have. This was a very sophisticated referral, since the oncologist, or cancer specialist, was anticipating the problem before
it could get out of control and require the use of powerful
narcotics. Chemotherapy causes severe nausea and vomiting,
and though Judith experienced much less of that than expected,
the doctor believed she would soon experience a lot of pain as
the cancer moved to different organs. Even with chemotherapy
and radiation, Judith was not expected to live more than six
months.

I taught Judith QR. She completed the full chemotherapy
and radiation program, and at the same time became very excited about the QR concept. She developed a remarkable will
to live and is indeed alive today, five years after her surgery.
Her cancer is in complete remission. I cannot argue that QR
brought about the remission; it was probably the chemotherapy
and radiation. But it is notable that most people with similar
cases die in six months despite such treatments. Certainly QR
helped convince Judith that although she needed the help of
doctors and medicine, she retained control of her body and
could develop her own will to survive. Judith now specializes
in cancer counseling, and QR is an important part of her approach.

Her case contrasts sharply with that of Molly, a 62-year-old woman who had undergone surgery for ovarian cancer, but not before the disease had spread to her liver. Molly was put on a long course of chemotherapy and radiation and began to develop severe pain problems, so her oncologist administered narcotic painkillers. He referred her to me when he became concerned that she was addicted to Demerol, a powerful narcotic similar to morphine.

I attempted to teach Molly QR, hoping not only to reduce the amount of medication she required, but to help her deal with her overall situation. Sadly, Molly never accepted the idea that she could have any mastery over her body or responsibility for her own health. She was entirely dependent on doctors and believed that she could be helped only by taking more pills. Her belief system just didn't allow for the possibility that her brain could regulate much of what happened in her body.

Within a few months Molly was dead. Her referral came too late for me to help her by teaching her self-regulation. Had the referral been made earlier I believe I could have helped Molly significantly, if not prolonging her life, then at least minimizing the amount of narcotics she had to take. People who learn QR require vastly lower levels of such drugs because, as they develop their sense of self-mastery, they become able to detach themselves somewhat from their pain. As later chapters will explain, they also learn not to brace against it, a natural reaction that often makes pain problems worse.

A traditional medical education trains doctors to prescribe drugs or surgery, and these techniques are often appropriate for such problems as infections, injuries, poisoning, congenital defects or tumors. Medication and surgical intervention are less useful for treating many stress-related ailments, however. To deal with the problems of chronic stress, the six-second QR technique emphasizes skills, rather than pills. After I developed QR, rather than give my patients a prescription with instructions for a pharmacist, I gave them instructions to enhance their understanding of QR and help them acquire automaticity in the QR skill. This book will serve the same purpose for you. So that you can understand how QR works and why it is so beneficial, the following chapters will provide a more detailed description of how stress produces illness.

4. How Stress Makes Us Sick

The idea that the stress and strain of living, particularly the stress and strain of emotional events, are the major factors underlying the production of stress-related symptoms, has been popularized by Friedman and Rosenman's *Type A Behavior and Your Heart* and by a widely used "life-events questionnaire" developed by Dr. Thomas Holmes and Dr. Richard Rahe. Their questionnaire, reproduced below, lists forty-two life events with assigned "life-event change unit" values. Holmes and Rahe's research has demonstrated that if a person accumulates more than 300 life-event change units during a six-month period, there is a high probability that he or she will experience a significant emotional or physical illness.

You can score yourself now on the life-events questionnaire to see how many points you have accumulated over the last six months. You will note that not all of the forty-two items for which life-event change units have been assigned are experiences that most people would consider "bad." Some life events, such as outstanding achievements, vacations, or marriages, though positive in many ways, nonetheless contribute to the accumulation of stress in our bodies that eventually produces physical symptoms.

Life-Events Questionnaire

WORK	LCU
Being fired from work	47
Retirement from work	45
Major business adjustment	39
Changing to different line of work	36
Major change in work responsibilities	29
Trouble with boss	23
Major change in working conditions	20

PERSONAL	
Major personal injury or illness	53
Outstanding personal achievement	28
Major revision of personal habits	24
Major change in recreation	19
Major change in church activities	19
Major change in sleeping habits	16
Major change in eating habits	15
Vacation	13

FINANCIAL	
Major change in financial state	38
Mortgage or loan over $10,000	31
Mortgage foreclosure	30
Mortgage or loan less than $10,000	17

FAMILY	LCU
Death of a spouse	100
Divorce	73
Marital separation	65
Death of a close family member	63
Marriage	50
Marital reconciliation	45
Major change in health of family	44
Pregnancy	40
Addition of new family member	39
Major change in arguments with spouse	35
Son or daughter leaving home	29
In-law troubles	29
Wife starting or ending work	26
Major change in family get-togethers	15

SOCIAL

Detention in jail	63
Sexual difficulties	39
Death of a close friend	37
Start or end of formal schooling	26
Major change in living conditions	25
Changing to a new school	20
Change in residence	20
Change in social activities	18
Minor violations of the law	11

Your total_____

Recently, scientists have begun to recognize that adverse stressors are not confined to life events or emotional stress, but include chemical and physical factors as well. An example of a common chemical stressor is the caffeine in coffee and cola drinks, a nervous-system stimulant that makes many people jittery, irritable and more susceptible to stress reactions. The table below lists several emotional stressors, as well as a number of chemical and physical factors that are increasingly cited as contributors to excessive activation of some of the body's arousal mechanisms.

Stressors

Chemical	*Physical*	*Emotional*
sugar	inactivity	fear
caffeine	trauma	anger
nicotine	pregnancy	guilt
alcohol	infections	intense joy
salt	excess work	
smog	weather	
DDT, etc.	erratic sleep habits	

Some Stress Beneficial

Before proceeding with a discussion of how stress makes us sick, it is important to establish that some forms of stress are healthy and crucial for productive behavior. Dr. Hans Selye, a famous pioneer in understanding how stress produces symptoms and illness, first made this point in his 1974 book, *Stress*

Without Distress. He reasoned that it is as stressful to put a thoroughbred out to pasture when it's accustomed to racing every day as it would be to shock a turtle to force it to run fast. Indeed in real life, we know that retirement is often very stressful for a busy executive.

Most inner organs in the body receive nerve control signals from the two branches of what is termed the autonomic nervous system. The parasympathetic branch has a calming and energy-conserving effect and tends to dominate when we are relaxed or in a low arousal state such as sleep. The sympathetic branch tends to activate and increase tension levels and dominates when we are excited, stressed, or in a high arousal state. Most stress-management, meditation and relaxation programs seek to lower arousal by decreasing the level of activity in the sympathetic system. The problem with this approach is that it ignores the need to maintain a healthy level of stress. People need to learn skills that will enable them to adjust their stress and tension levels from high to low to suit the task at hand. In subsequent chapters, we shall see that QR answers this need.

Five Phases of the Stress Response Sequence

In this chapter, we will explore the basic mechanisms underlying stress and arousal, which involve essentially five phases:

1. The fight-or-flight emergency response, or alarm reaction.
2. The general adaptation syndrome.
3. Dysponesis, or trying too hard.
4. A state of helplessness and hopelessness.
5. Irregularity of the "body-clock" system.

An understanding of these phases will help explain how unregulated excessive arousal may contribute to as much as 70 to 90 percent of the illnesses treated by physicians.

Alarm Signals of Stress

The first of the five phases comprising the body's stress response sequence, the emergency response, has already been introduced. An expanded list of the initial stages of the emergency response is presented below. This series of changes is set off by two body activities—first, brain activation of the sympathetic branch of the nervous system, then release of the hormone adrenaline from the medulla of the adrenal glands, which are located just above the kidneys. These initial stages of the emergency response are all highly useful if you are faced with a real threat that requires you to fight or run away. When the response is called up inappropriately and excessively, however, it can lead to any of the symptoms listed in chapter 1.

Initial Stages of the Emergency Response

1. Cue, or stimulus, perceived as threatening.
2. Perking up attention—orienting and focusing on the cue. Pupils dilate.
3. Tensing muscles to fight or run.
4. Catching or holding breath or panting.
5. Clenching jaws.
6. Constriction or decrease of blood flow to hands, feet, gut.
7. Increase of heart rate.
8. Increase of blood pressure.
9. Blood clotting promoted.
10. Release of glucose for energy.

An explanation of the mechanism presumed to underlie the classic migraine headache, which affects up to 20 percent of the Western population, illustrates how the events of the emergency response produce body discomfort.

The cue initiating a migraine headache may be emotional,

such as a response to a perceived stressful event, or physical, perhaps triggered by a stressor food—chocolate and peanut butter are common ones. In individuals who do not experience migraine headaches, stage 6 of the emergency response, as shown above, is constriction of blood flow to the hands, feet, intestines and stomach, with a redirection of blood to the deeper skeletal muscles that would be used for running or fighting if it were appropriate. In the migraine-prone individual, however, stage 6 also produces constriction of the arteries carrying blood to the brain and eyes. The resulting reduction in the flow of blood to the brain produces the various early symptoms of migraine, such as flashing lights or blurred vision.

The eyes and brain are greedy organs, together requiring about one-third of the output of blood from the heart. Natural protective mechanisms assure them an adequate blood supply. When this supply is reduced by constriction of the blood vessels, a "fuse" chemical located in the walls of the arteries is released and effectively shuts off the constricting influence of the sympathetic nerves that control all arteries.

With the activation of the sympathetic nerves eliminated, the vessels supplying blood to the brain overrelax and become engorged with blood, almost like bicycle tires pumped up to the size of truck tires. The brain is assured an adequate blood supply, but pain receptors located in the walls of the stretching vessels produce head pains so severe that they can be incapacitating. Classic migraine headache, then, results when the smooth muscles lining arteries respond to stage 6 of the emergency response; the neural tissue of the brain itself is not involved. (If people who've acquired automaticity in the QR technique quickly do a QR as soon as a warning symptom appears, they are frequently able to abort the progress of a migraine headache into the pain phase.)

Consequences of the General Adaptation Syndrome

Most of us recover from many of the symptoms—such as headache, constipation, gassiness, palpitations or nausea—that can develop from overactivation of the emergency response. By contrast, the symptoms resulting from the second phase in the stress response sequence, the general adaptation syndrome, frequently are irreversible. They include severe kidney damage, heart attacks, strokes and even cancer—conditions that require the most advanced medications and surgical technology that medical science can provide.

The role of general adaptation syndrome arousal mechanism in producing illness has been established through the monumental investigations of Dr. Hans Selye, a famous pioneer in understanding stress-related illness. His findings have gained acceptance by the medical community only during the last decade.

The general adaptation syndrome—G.A.S. for short—has three identifiable stages. The first is the *alarm stage*, another name for the fight-or-flight emergency response, which involves the sympathetic nervous system and the secretion of adrenaline from the middle part of the adrenal glands.

When the alarm, or emergency response, is chronically activated, the pituitary gland, located in the brain, secretes a hormone called ACTH. This in turn causes the outer layer of the adrenal glands, the adrenal cortex, to secrete hormones called steroids. The initial response of the body to steroids in the bloodstream is a protective reaction to prevent inflammation, a term describing an excessive and ineffective reaction of the body's defense system. Rashes, hives, many symptoms of the common cold, and the joint pain and swelling of arthritis are all examples of inflammation. The body's protective reaction against inflammation marks the second stage of the G.A.S., the *resistance stage*, which follows quickly after the alarm stage. It is the resistance component of the adrenal steroids that has led physicians to use them as drugs to treat shock and reduce inflammatory processes that can occur in any organ of the body.

Unfortunately, if steroids—whether administered for medical reasons or produced as the result of excessive stress—remain at too high a level for too long a time, undesirable consequences develop in what Selye perceived as the third stage of the G.A.S., the *exhaustion stage*. At this time, we can only guess how long it takes for a person to cross over into the exhaustion stage, but Holmes and Rahe's work suggests that when chronic activation of the alarm stage persists for somewhere around six months, movement into the exhaustion stage occurs. The consequences of the exhaustion stage are so detrimental that physicians have to be extremely cautious in their use of steroids; they do not like to administer steroids to suppress ineffective defense mechanisms for longer than ten days.

Experiments comparing the effects of steroids administered as drugs and steroids produced as the result of excessive distress have demonstrated that the two are equally capable of producing the following medical problems:

1. An acceleration of hardening of the arteries and increased susceptibility to clogged or ruptured arteries, heart attacks and strokes.

When healthy people exercise, minute tears develop in the delicate inner lining of the arteries, which is a layer about one cell thick. If not repaired, these tears could lead to hemorrhaging into the artery wall. In an unstressed individual, cell division takes place in the cells adjacent to the rip, and a new cell is slipped in to repair the defect, a process taking approximately ninety minutes. In the chronically stressed individual producing significant amounts of adrenal steroids, however, the required patch job has to be much faster, because the adrenaline in his blood stream raises his blood pressure and heart rate, exaggerating the tendency to hemorrhage. It's like a water system under very high pressure: a leak has to be mended rapidly to prevent loss of the water supply, whereas a similar leak in a system under low pressure would not be as devastating.

To accomplish the needed repair quickly, the body plugs the rip with a small gob of cholesterol, a fatty substance that normally circulates in our blood stream. But as these cholesterol plaques accumulate, they begin to clog the artery or they cause a weakening of the artery wall. The damaged arteries may become completely blocked or rupture, producing a heart attack if a vessel of the heart wall is involved, or a stroke if the affected vessel carries blood to the brain.

2. Cancer. Although steroids are used to treat various forms of cancer, in some people these same steroids increase the body's tendency to spontaneously develop cancer cells. Each

day, millions of cells in the body undergo *mitosis*, or duplication, either to repair a malfunction or to renew cells that have reached their normal life expectancy. Inevitably an occasional mistake occurs, and an abnormal cell results. In normal individuals, special white cells called T-lymphocytes circulating in the bloodstream destroy such cells; this is part of the body's defense system, which prevents abnormal cells from growing into significant tumor masses. We now know that physical and chemical stressors, such as nicotine and insecticides, enhance the chances that cell division will produce an abnormal cell, and thus increase the chances that an individual's T-lymphocyte defense mechanisms will not be adequate. If the individual is under constant stress and showing symptoms of the G.A.S., two factors are then operating to increase his risk of cancer.

3. A lack of what is popularly thought of as "resistance." When we say, "I caught the flu because I let myself get run down and was under too much stress," we are making a common-sense interpretation of the exhaustion stage of the G.A.S., which reduces the number of another type of circulating white cells in the blood that normally defend against invading bacteria or viruses.

4. Ulcers in the section of the intestine below the stomach, a condition that has long been associated with the stress of high-pressure jobs. Such ulcers also are frequently seen in patients who have been receiving steroids for an inflammatory condition.

5. Irreversible kidney damage that may lead to kidney failure and eventually the need for dialysis or a kidney transplant. Kidney damage can also lead to the development of malignant hypertension, which accounts for about 10 percent of high blood pressure cases.

Most of the potentially irreversible conditions linked to the G.A.S. (many of which can be treated with medication and surgery) can be caused by factors other than stress, but most physicians would agree that stress usually plays a significant role. It is difficult to place a percentage figure on the incidence of these problems in medical practice, but an estimate of 20 to 30 percent would probably be accurate. As the G.A.S. produced by chronic stress is better understood, one sees the importance of using QR as a strategy for preventing illness by interrupting the alarm phase of the stress response sequence when it is inappropriate.

Dysponetic Efforts—"Grin and Bear It"

Imagine yourself sitting in a dental chair while the dentist drills a cavity after failing to achieve adequate pain blockage with a local anesthetic. The tendency of most people in this situation is to avoid complaining unless the pain is overwhelming. Instead we brace our skeletal muscles, seeking a defensive position, in an attempt to minimize the pain sensation. This muscle bracing is "faulty effort," because it actually increases the pain. Such faulty bracing efforts have been given the name *dysponesis* by George Whatmore, M.D., of the University of Washington, who has been studying the phenomenon for over twenty-five years.

Having been taught throughout life to try hard to succeed, to try to be brave, or to "grin and bear it," many people adopt a similar strategy for overcoming symptoms or pain problems. But Type A mental efforts have a negative effect on inner body organs that are diseased or painful. For an individual experiencing low back pain, for example, trying too hard to overcome the discomfort only puts the muscles of the lower back into greater spasm, increasing the pain in a vicious circle. Dysponesis is a trap that our clever Type A minds have created for us—they have forgotten how to maintain Type B bodies.

Dysponetic efforts are universally associated with all distressing symptoms and pain, whether resulting from stress mechanisms or other organic causes. A large part of the nonprescription drug industry is founded on the principle of dysponesis. When you come down with the flu, you probably go to a drugstore and buy numerous over-the-counter remedies, hoping to recover without bothering your busy doctor, who you feel might not be able to help anyway. The Food and Drug Administration estimates that 70 percent of such medications are ineffective. Popular self-help books for various medical problems suggest a vast variety of solutions, but seem to over-look the underlying problem of dysponetic faulty bracing efforts. Such books often emphasize an exercise program or other regimen to solve a problem. But usually, after reading the book, people *try too hard* and aggravate their conditions.

Healthy people exhibit a capacity to cope effectively with stressors, usually regaining a quieting state within a relatively short time after emergency response episodes. This inherent quieting response allows their bodies to restore needed energy reserves, preparing them for subsequent arousal periods. By contrast, most of us who are predisposed to stress illnesses generally recover a state of balance much more slowly, if at all. We tend to maintain excessively high levels of activity in both muscle and hormonal systems. Although such biological factors as organic disease, tissue damage and hostile environmental conditions can contribute to such a "recovery deficit," most stress-prone individuals seem to gradually learn to override their inherent quieting mechanisms. My colleagues and I have observed that children can reacquire the quieting state much more readily than adults. Apparently the arousal response in adults can become so routinized that it has all the characteristics of an acquired, seemingly automatic behavior pattern, and people come to regard the aroused state as normal.

When people become accustomed to constant arousal, the concepts of relaxation and calm lose their meaning. Stress sufferers may report that states of relaxation and calm are elusive, contend that they really should be avoided if one is to perform well and "make the most of life," or claim to have achieved them when sensors attached to their bodies indicate otherwise. In fact, these people frequently experience discomfort when they achieve genuine physiological quieting, which suggests how deeply ingrained their "dysponetic expectations" have become. They feel uneasy when their bodies aren't "hyped up" by the usual sensations of stress. This, again, is the "after-the-battle phenomenon"; when part of the battle against stress has been won, people feel worse for a time as buried stresses surface. (Athletes often do not experience the pain of injuries during competition, but the pain surfaces when the event is over.) Unless people who are accustomed to chronic stress have a strong commitment to achieving self-regulation, they will resist quieting, but if they persist in their training, their discomfort will pass.

Breaking the Dysponetic Circle

QR breaks the vicious circle of dysponesis by including an inner sense of humor, a state of passive alertness and a sense of looking within—none of which can be achieved by trying too hard.

Dysponetic behaviors, or ingrained faulty-bracing habits, require grim determination and accentuate the muscle tensing and tendency to jaw clenching of the early phases of the emergency response. Maintaining one's sense of humor is one effective strategy for interrupting dysponetic tendencies, as described in Norman Cousins' recent best-seller, *Anatomy of an Illness*.

Cousins had contracted a disease that was causing the connective tissue in his spine to disintegrate. He had trouble moving his limbs or even turning over in bed, and at one point, his jaws were almost locked. Cousins was subjected—with grim determination on his part and on the part of his physicians—to an elaborate set of diagnostic procedures in an expensive hospital, but in time he became fed up because the physicians weren't coming up with effective solutions. Indeed, he was told that his chance of recovery was 1 in 500.

Cousins was familiar with Hans Selye's research into stress and knew that negative emotions could produce negative chemical changes in the body. He began to wonder whether positive emotions—love, hope, faith, laughter, confidence and the will to live—might produce positive changes.

Cousins left the oppressive atmosphere of the hospital for a less costly hotel room. Concerned that toxifying painkillers were further debilitating his body's capacity to recover, he stopped taking them and substituted massive doses of ascorbic acid, or vitamin C, for the drugs that had been administered to combat inflammation. At the same time, he began to spend many hours watching classic comic movies or listening to his nurse read to him from humor books.

"It worked," he reported. "I made the joyous discovery that ten minutes of genuine belly laughter had an anesthetic effect and would give me at least two hours of pain-free sleep. When the pain-killing effect of the laughter wore off, we would switch on the motion-picture projector again, and, not infrequently, it would lead to another pain-free sleep interval."

To determine whether the laughter was having an actual physiologic effect on his body, Cousins had sedimentation-rate readings taken before and after the laughter episodes. In this diagnostic test, the rate at which red blood cells settle in a test tube is measured; the speed is proportionate to the severity of many illnesses. In each of the tests made after Cousins' periods of laughter, there was a drop in the sedimentation rate, and these drops held and were cumulative. With his self-prescription of laughter and ascorbic acid, Cousins' condition steadily improved until he essentially was recovered, except for some lingering pain in one shoulder and in his knees. Cousins' demonstration that "laughter is the best medicine" is paralleled in the six-second QR technique, in which an ability to maintain an inner sense of humor—directed in part at oneself—is an important component.

Letting Go to Get Well

Learning to give in to the wisdom of the mind and the inner balance in one's body is another successful technique for interrupting dysponetic tendencies; it is the opposite of trying too hard. As already described, when people working with biofeedback instruments try too hard to achieve control of an inner body system, they fail, because in trying too hard they make their stress systems all the more active. One of the most important aspects of coaching people to acquire self-regulation skills is teaching them that they don't have to approach the task like Olympic athletes. When they stop making excessive efforts and adopt an attitude of passive attention to what's happening in their bodies, they soon succeed in producing the desired result, as registered by the biofeedback instrument.

The creation of a state of passive alertness and looking within oneself, which cannot be achieved by trying too hard, is a common thread among self-regulation techniques throughout history. The ancient Chinese philosopher Lao-tzu captured the essence of this inner awareness that opens greater vistas for body balance and personal growth:

> There is no need to run outside
> For better seeing,
> Nor to peer from a window. Rather abide
> At the center of your being;
> For the more you leave it, the less you learn.
> Search your heart and see
> If he is wise who takes each turn;
> The way to do is to be.*

Helplessness and Hopelessness

As they pass through the first three stages of the arousal mechanism sequence—the alarm or emergency response, the general adaptation syndrome, and dysponesis—most people develop a sense of futility that is in itself stressful. While psychiatrists label this state depression, it can best be described as a feeling of helplessness and hopelessness that may persist despite efforts by physicians or by the individual himself to reverse it.

In the midst of this feeling of helplessness and hopelessness, a person may think over and over, "I can't continue; I can't do it." Such a state is a prelude to psychological and physiological events that can lead to suicide. Dr. Elizabeth Kübler-Ross has extensively examined this process in her widely acclaimed books on death and dying.

Some degree of helplessness and hopelessness is normal in all of us when faced with the loss of a friend or loved one, a body function, or a potential capability (when, on entering middle age, a person realizes that he or she will never reach the top career level, for example). When psychiatrists can clearly

*Lao-tzu. *The Way of Life*. Translated by Witter Bynner. New York: Capricorn Books, 1944.

identify such a loss, they classify the person as having an *exogenous depression*, which usually responds to supportive measures and the cure of time. When the state of helplessness and hopelessness results from some imbalance in hormonal or neuronal functioning, the diagnosis is *endogenous depression*, and some form of drug therapy must be used to restore normal balance.

By interrupting the earlier phases of the stress response sequence, the use of QR can keep chronically stressed people from reaching the point where they become depressed. If someone does reach the depression stage, however, no self-regulation technique is effective, because people who feel helpless and hopeless tend to become so unmotivated that they cannot make the effort to practice. This is not unlike the common case of someone who, as the result of a stroke, has lost coordinated movement or even all movement of skeletal muscles in some portion of his body, yet won't work at physical therapy and other treatments. If the person were motivated, retraining whatever muscle function remains could help him regain some of his capacity. Regrettably, many patients entering the exhaustion stage of the G.A.S. become incapable of even meager efforts to help themselves. They give up, losing the desire to recover and sometimes even the desire to live.

Depression does not mean simply being "down." Some people experiencing helplessness and hopelessness appear lethargic and exhausted, but others, including some of the depressives who are most difficult to treat, show their depression by becoming agitated or destructive. In either case, the first three phases of the arousal mechanism sequence—alarm, G.A.S. and dysponesis—are activated, often at an unconscious level. People suffering from a state of despair should not proceed with the QR training program, but should immediately consult their family physician for possible referral to a psychologist or psychiatrist who can carefully evaluate feelings of depression and thoughts of suicide.

Summary of Possible Pathways

As we experience pain and suffering from symptoms of either the acute emergency response or the G.A.S., we enter one of two pathways. The first, the dysponetic pathway of bracing against the pain, creates a vicious circle in which we experience even more emergency response because the more we brace against pain, the more we feel pain sensations. The second, the exhaustion stage of the G.A.S., leads to a sensation of helplessness and hopelessness that may or may not respond to treatment by a physician.

As Figure 2 indicates, if we add up the medical complaints arising from the acute emergency response and the general adaptation syndrome, we find that stress is either a causal factor or significantly worsens a problem by reactivating the stress

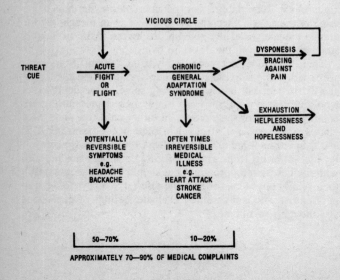

Figure 2

cycle through dysponesis in 70 to 90 percent of all medical complaints.

Figure 3 clarifies this circular process and shows how dysponesis is a central problem once we get caught in a situation in which we experience body symptoms and pain. Clearly any approach that interrupts this vicious circle should promote recovery. Minor tranquilizers are effective in chemically interrupting the initial phase of the arousal reaction and can be used in short-term situations, but while these measures may be initially effective, they permit people to take on more stress that can override the interruptive effect of the tranquilizer, permitting an even more vicious stress cycle to begin. A self-regulation technique like QR, which can help people develop adaptive behaviors that restore normal inner balance in the body, is clearly preferable. An individual moves from adaptive homeostasis, or inner balance, to a situation in which potentially reversible symptoms result from the emergency response fight-or-flight, and finally to a breakdown phase in which irreversible

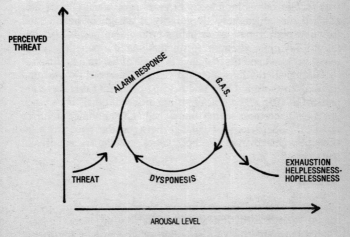

Figure 3

symptoms develop. The goal of QR is to interrupt the process before the symptoms can create life-threatening consequences.

Body Rhythms and Stress

One remaining factor is important in understanding how stress makes us sick: that is its ability to interfere with our "body-clock" system. The inner balance of the body is not constant, but varies according to a set of inner biological clocks that operate as a master timekeeper, allocating the body's resources for optimal functioning. In health, an appearance of stability cloaks an inner symphony of biological rhythms that cover a broad time spectrum: fractions of a second for biochemical reactions and nerve impulses; about a second for the heart rhythm; ninety minutes for the rapid eye movement (REM) cycle of dreaming during the night; a corresponding ninety-minute cycle of alert activity versus daydreaming during the day; a major twenty-four-hour rest-activity cycle; the twenty-seven-day menstrual cycle, and finally, the lengthy cycle of a single lifespan. The importance of biological rhythms to health was recognized as long as 2400 years ago, when Hippocrates advised his colleagues, "Regularity is a sign of health, and irregular body functions or habits promote an unsalutary condition. Pay close attention to fluctuations in a patient's symptoms, his good and his bad days in times of health and illness."

Biological rhythms alter the balance between arousal and quieting in the mind and body. Most of us find that there are parts of the day when our minds are aroused, other times when our mental alertness seems diminished and our bodies are more aroused, and periods of balance between the two. Irregular schedules that disrupt the body-clock system are significant stressors.

JET LAG

One such external disruption that has drawn attention to the role of biological rhythms in stress-related illnesses is "jet lag." This is the four- to five-day period of fatigue and adjustment needed to resynchronize the inner body-clock system with the activity cycle of a new time zone after a transcontinental flight. Diplomats, athletes and others who travel frequently because of their professions are beginning to anticipate and deal with jet lag with a variety of techniques, including artificially adopting the destination's time schedule a week before departure, incorporating intermediate stopovers into transcontinental travel, or allowing for an adjustment period at the destination point before performing or making critical decisions.

A recently recognized related stress problem is the "jet fatigue" experienced by flight crews, who experience such symptoms as headache, burning eyes, blurred vision, gastrointestinal problems, loss of appetite, shortness of breath, excessive sweating, insomnia and nightmares. That many of these conditions have already been identified as symptoms of chronic activation of the emergency response dramatically underscores the fact that tampering with our inborn biological rhythms can seriously affect the normal balance between arousal and quieting mechanisms and produce physical and emotional problems.

CONSISTENT SCHEDULES AND STRESS

"Night people" differ from "day people" in using a different set of cues to synchronize their body rhythms with their environment. They set their clocks for different hours when work schedules allow and respond to different social cues—night people tend to prefer the kinds of social activities that go on at night, while day people favor those that take place during the day. Scientists are not agreed on whether one is naturally a "day" or "night" person. Some argue that you can choose to be either, as long as you maintain a consistent schedule. But recent findings indicate that night people have a much slower rise of steroids in the bloodstream than day people do and thus don't really become active till much later in the day. They are night people biologically.

Studies have revealed that shift workers who work five nights a week and then attempt to become active during the day on weekends experience many of the symptoms of jet lag. If you deviate from your normal schedule of waking and sleep-

ing, your internal biological rhythms "desynchronize" and begin to drift, gaining or losing a few minutes each day. This
condition, known as free-running, has been advanced as a possible explanation for certain forms of insomnia that may be
associated with symptoms of depression. If a person has consciously or unconsciously begun to ignore the regular pattern
of his life because of stress or conflict, his underlying rhythm
structure may begin to free run so that his body is eventually
prepared for day activity during the night and for night rest
during the day. When the rhythm drifts progressively, consistently gaining a few minutes each day, insomnia is first
experienced at bedtime, then during the night and finally in
the early morning. The opposite progression is observed when
the free-running biological rhythms consistently lose a few
minutes each day. In the absence of a consistent trend, virtually
any insomnia pattern can be explained by this mechanism. This
phenomenon has been documented in behaviorally stressed
monkeys, which at the same time exhibited a variety of other
stress-related symptoms.

Many people can "set" a waking time with their inner biological clocks, consistently awakening one or two minutes
before their bedside alarms ring. Many people can do this
regardless of the time for which the clock is set. The individual
is giving himself a tiny verbal suggestion, and his brain is
linking it to some biological alarm mechanism within the body.
It is not yet understood whether this capacity is genetic or
acquired, but it is remarkable that such a minor suggestion
before bedtime is able to determine when a quiet, sleeping
person will become aroused and awaken. It highlights the great
power of the brain to control the body, a power which, on the
one hand, renders us susceptible to stress diseases and on the
other, allows us to achieve the quieting state that minimizes
stress disease.

THE BIORHYTHM FAD

It is important to distinguish real biological rhythms, which
can be measured in a laboratory, from the popular theory of

"biorhythms." Biorhythm theory claims that we are subject to an intrinsic twenty-three day physical rhythm, a twenty-eight day emotional sensitivity rhythm, and a thirty-three day mental performance rhythm, all set in motion at the moment of birth. Widespread promotion of the biorhythm theory as fact, in books and articles and through personalized computer predictions and pocket calculators, has obscured the distinction between the speculative biorhythm theory and the demonstrated biological rhythms of the body.

RECHARGING BODY BATTERIES

Earlier in this chapter, I discussed the importance of the adrenal steroid hormones in producing the physical and mental symptoms associated with the stages of the general adaptation syndrome. The inner biological rhythms depend heavily on a twenty-four-hour rise and fall in blood steroids as a signal system for recharging the energy stores of the brain and body. When the regularity of the steriod signal system is obscured by feelings of helplessness and hopelessness or by stress activation of the general adaptation syndrome, illness often ensues.

The steroid body clock dictates that at some points during the day arousal is facilitated and at others quieting is facilitated allowing recharging of our energy stores. Normally, one's biological rhythms cycle could be represented graphically by a series of connected **S**s laid on their sides. Each **S** would represent a twenty-four-hour period, the low arc of the curve, or trough, corresponding to the period of quieting (night), the high arc to the period of arousal (day). The alternating highs and lows appear in a state of balance, one equal to the next, with occasional small, sharp upswings, or peaks, superimposed on the high points of the basic rhythm curve, indicating emergency responses that last a relatively brief time—either until the precipitating threat has been resolved, or until, in the event of only a perceived threat, balance has been restored through a mechanism like the six-second QR technique.

It is at the low points of the biological rhythms cycle that the steroid systems—the body's "stress batteries"—are recharged. The periods during which these systems are recharged represent times of unusual vulnerability in normal people. These low points usually occur sometime between three and five-thirty in the morning in day-active people, and a worldwide peak incidence of heart attacks, strokes, heightened pain sensitivity and other medical problems during this period in the twenty-four-hour cycle has been documented. The famous film director Ingmar Bergman depicted this phenomenon in his movie *Hour of the Wolf*, in which the tortured hero suffered insomnia, anxiety and pain that grew worse during the early hours of the morning.

Because the low points of the biological rhythms cycle are periods of increased vulnerability, it may seem an ideal strategy to reduce these troughs by maintaining a higher activity or arousal level during the twenty-four hour cycle. Just the opposite is the case, however, as noted in my discussion of jet fatigue. When a person undergoes chronic activation of the arousal mechanisms, the arousal periods occur too frequently, never returning to the normal baseline, until the troughs of the normal biological rhythm—the recharging periods—no longer occur. This is often the situation of a person who feels helpless and hopeless and suffers from insomnia. He does not permit the daily steroid cycle to drop to the low levels normal during the "hour of the wolf" and progressively does not recharge his "stress batteries." As a result, he progresses to the exhaustion stage of the general adaptation syndrome.

QR to Reinforce Body Rhythms

By reducing inappropriate activation of the hormonal and neuronal systems, the QR technique encourages regular functioning of the internal biological rhythm system. An important part of learning the Quieting Reflex is practicing it at many points during the day and even when awake during the night, so that it becomes automatic at any point in the twenty-four-hour biological cycle.

In this chapter, I've explained the five phases of the stress response sequence, the basic mechanisms through which stress produces illness. In the next chapter, we'll explore those factors that determine which of the many illnesses that have been linked with stress will afflict a particular individual.

5. The Compass Points of Healthy and Unhealthy Stress

People learning the QR technique often ask questions such as, "How come gut problems run in my family?" or "Since most of my male relatives had early heart attacks, can I expect to have one?" or "I read the book on 'Type A' people having heart trouble, but how does this explain all the other stress-related problems, like headaches and nausea, that I experience?"

Friedman and Rosenman's introduction of the concept of Type A and Type B behavior forced scientists to begin thinking about the stress of life and its consequences for the body. They began to examine the mechanisms of stress, exploring the important findings of earlier researchers, including Claude Bernard, Walter Cannon and Hans Selye, which indicate that each of us activates body tension levels according to our heredity, early upbringing and life experiences. Depending on the individual, too much of a Type A mind can produce any of a wide variety of mental or somatic symptoms. The next question to ask is: How do stress mechanisms produce so many different symptoms in people, and what determines which symptoms a particular person will experience?

A Hierarchy of Reactions

According to one widely accepted theory, when we experience inappropriate activation of the fight-or-flight response some of us are "skin reactors," some "heart reactors" and some "gut reactors." The reason for these different patterns is not yet understood, though they probably relate to heredity or early experience, but each of us has a hierarchy of systems in which we develop symptoms if we undergo the stages of the emergency response excessively. Almost everyone can tell you what happens to him first when he experiences stress. Skin reactors may say, "I blush," or "I begin to break out in hives or acne." Heart reactors are aware that their blood pressure shoots up, their heart rate increases, and they develop palpitations. Some gut reactors say, "I get butterflies in my stomach," while others develop cramps or what doctors call *tenesmus*, an urgent but frequently ineffectual need to defecate, which is often unrelated to any real biological need.

One such "gut reactor" was Bernice, a 54-year-old housewife. For twenty years, Bernice had felt the need to go to the bathroom fifteen to twenty times a day, and her bowel pattern alternated unpredictably between diarrhea and constipation and cramping. Her entire life was constrained by her need to stay close to a bathroom. She had never been on an airplane, for example, because she couldn't be sure that one of the lavatories would be free at all times.

Because people are generally embarrassed to talk about such problems, most don't realize how widespread they are, but conditions like Bernice's afflict between 15 and 20 percent of the population. Physicians are well aware of this, as are the drug companies, which have produced a vast array of medications that are supposed to control the problem. Unfortunately, at the dosage level where medication begins to regulate the stomach and lower intestine, it usually begins to produce undesirable side effects as well.

Bernice had consulted many specialists in gastroenterology and had received many medications, particularly antispasm medications, as well as moderate doses of Valium. Within seven to ten days of each change in medication, she would experience relief from her symptoms, but it never lasted more than four or five days. One doctor had suggested that she start wearing diapers—a common way of dealing with bowel problems in geriatric patients—but she had resisted the idea.

Finally a gastroenterologist had referred Bernice to me because her pattern of feeling relief each time a new medicine offered hope suggested that she might be a "placebo responder"—someone who experiences symptom relief because of the expectation of symptom relief, whether a sugar pill or a truly active drug is administered. QR is a sound psychological and physiological approach to making "placebo response" a permanent behavior. It uses the incredible power of the mind—which the placebo response illustrates—to produce an ongoing positive effect on health.

I taught Bernice QR, focusing particularly on an exercise that you will learn called "the little warm blanket technique," in which she developed the image of a soothing little warm blanket that she could move to cover any area where she felt either cramping or a spasm leading to the sensation of needing to go to the bathroom. This technique proved incredibly effective. Eight months after I saw Bernice for the first time, she was able to fly across the country to visit her grandchildren. When she comes to see me each year for a checkup, Bernice always throws her arms around me, because she feels that what's happened to her is a miracle—but of course she did it for herself.

Four Pathways of Stress

The terms "gut reactor," "skin reactor" and "heart reactor" identify the systems in which we experience symptoms during the initial stages of the emergency response. A more complex theory, which I call "the compass points of healthy and unhealthy stress," seeks to explain more fully how a single factor—stress—can affect the myriad of health problems that physicians now acknowledge are stress related, and to suggest why particular individuals are susceptible to certain types of stress-related problems.

Thus far, we have viewed the whole body as being in an A/B status along the arousal dimensions for the mind and body. Actually, however, there are four interrelated mechanisms of control within the body, each of which is subject to over- or underarousal. They are: neurons, hormones, skeletal (voluntary) muscles and smooth muscles. The existence of these four basic "pathways of stress" was first clearly elucidated by Edgar Wilson, M.D., and Carol Schneider, Ph.D., of the University of Colorado at Boulder. I have elaborated their original theory into the "compass points of healthy and unhealthy stress," as illustrated in Figure 4, which shows these four stress pathways at the ends of arrows that can be thought of as the points of a compass.

The smooth muscles, indicated at the right, line the blood vessels of the body, most of the gastrointestinal tract including the stomach and intestines, and the air passageways of the lungs. Neurons, at the top of the figure, are the active communicating parts of the brain and nervous system. The skeletal muscles, at the left, are under voluntary control of the brain and move our eyes, our vocal chords and our skeleton. Hormones, shown at the bottom, are released from a variety of organs and are transmitted via the bloodstream to various target areas, where their effect is to increase or decrease activity. For example, adrenaline, secreted by the adrenal glands, causes the heart rate to speed up and the blood vessels in the extremities to constrict.

Figure 4 also shows two circles in the middle of the compass. The space between them represents a region of balance. The area beyond the outer circle represents a state of over-arousal, which includes overactivation of any of the four control mechanisms. The inner circle denotes a state of inadequate arousal, which includes reduced activation.

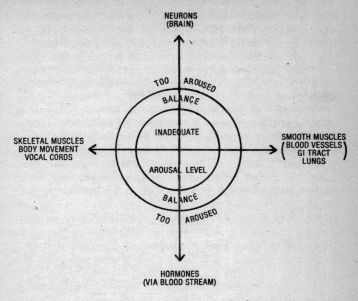

Figure 4

The initial arousal produced by the emergency response involves all four components, or "compass points," as indicated in Figure 5. Smooth-muscle arousal causes dilation of the pupils and constriction of blood flow to the hands and feet. Neuronal arousal involves increased vigilance and activation of the sympathetic nerves. Skeletal muscle activation leads to tensing muscles, including the diaphragm—and hence holding the breath—and clenching the jaws. Finally, hormonal activation involves pumping adrenaline into the bloodstream.

Are You a Clencher?

Overactivation of any one of the four stress pathways can lead to related mental or physical symptoms. As represented in

Figure 6, for example, overarousal of the skeletal muscles can lead to such problems as tension headache, backache, and some forms of tremor and whiplash. A case exemplifying this condition is that of Walter, a 44-year-old engineer, who came to me complaining of daily headaches on awakening that he experienced as constant pain, like a band around his head, or sometimes as a shooting pain in his neck. I diagnosed his problem as muscle contraction tension headache.

During our consultation, I examined the joints where the jaw is attached to the skull, which are called the temporomandibular joints, or TMJs for short. In such an examination, I put my fingers in front of the ears and feel the movement of the jawbone. About 20 percent of the population has difficulty with this joint, although not all of them get headaches. In

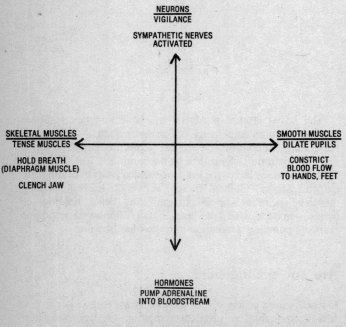

Figure 5

Walter's case, there was a definite abnormality, so I referred him to his dentist, who found that Walter also had a history of nocturnal bruxism, or teeth grinding during the night.

The dentist carried out a variety of procedures over six months, including grinding down Walter's teeth on one side to adjust the way they fit together and put the TMJs in balance. He then produced a molded bite plate to be worn at night to minimize the teeth grinding. Still Walter experienced no relief from his morning headaches, and the dentist referred him back to me.

After careful discussion with Walter, I became aware that when stressed, he overactivated his skeletal muscles. He was a real "clencher"—when he drove, he tended to clench the steering wheel, and he also unconsciously clenched his teeth whenever he got uptight.

Since jaw clenching is one of the stages of the emergency response, I taught Walter the QR technique, in which the stages of the emergency response are reversed. Step 4 of the QR entails

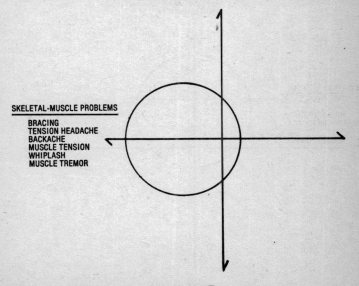

Figure 6

dropping the jaw to relieve pressure on the TMJs. Within weeks, Walter began to experience freedom from his awakening headaches. Occasionally he had a breakthrough headache, so I taught him to hold his chin with his fingers, do a QR, gently manipulate his jaw until he found a position that relieved his pain, and do another QR. Most of the time this made his headache disappear entirely.

Single and Combined Problems

Subsequent figures show the kinds of problems that result from overactivation of the remaining compass points. Figure 7 de-

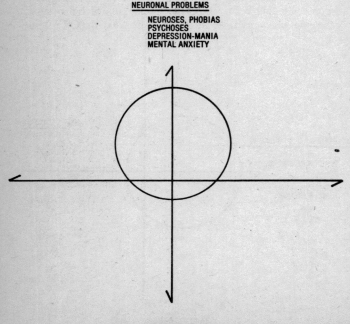

Figure 7

picts the results of excessive arousal of the neurons in the brain and nervous system. While even psychiatrists and neurologists don't fully understand the mechanisms involved in their production, problems from excessive nervous activation include such neurotic behaviors as obsessions, phobias and anxieties; psychotic conditions in which individuals lose touch with reality; and depressive conditions of helplessness and hopelessness.

Figure 8 shows problems resulting from excessive smooth-muscle arousal. These include about 90 percent of high blood pressure difficulties, irritable colon, nervous stomach, heartburn, nausea, fast heartbeat, some forms of asthma and migraine headaches. The way in which migraine headache is produced when the smooth muscles lining the arteries to the

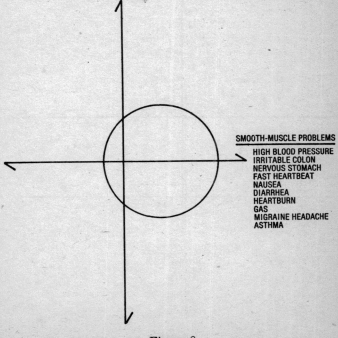

SMOOTH-MUSCLE PROBLEMS

HIGH BLOOD PRESSURE
IRRITABLE COLON
NERVOUS STOMACH
FAST HEARTBEAT
NAUSEA
DIARRHEA
HEARTBURN
GAS
MIGRAINE HEADACHE
ASTHMA

Figure 8

brain respond to stress has already been described.

Figure 9 shows some of the problems that result when the hormonal system is over- or underaroused, including thyroid problems, obesity, excessive sweating, some forms of hair loss, menopausal problems, various skin problems, and some forms of male impotence.

Many people experience problems resulting from the over- or underarousal of more than one system. Examples could fill a medical textbook, but two will suffice here. A person who suffers from migraine headaches once or twice a month, with muscle contraction or tension headaches in between—probably resulting from worry and tension over when the next migraine attack will occur—shows hyperarousal of both the skeletal

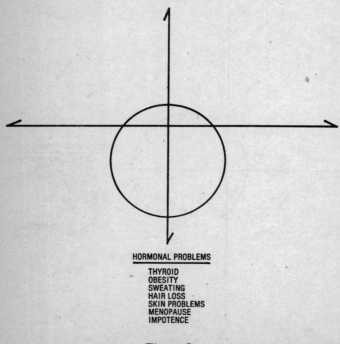

HORMONAL PROBLEMS

THYROID
OBESITY
SWEATING
HAIR LOSS
SKIN PROBLEMS
MENOPAUSE
IMPOTENCE

Figure 9

muscles and the smooth muscles lining the arteries that carry blood to the brain. (See Figure 10, dotted lines). It is likely that the tension headaches enhance the onset of more migraines than the individual might otherwise experience.

The solid circle in Figure 10 shows a situation in which a person has excessive arousal in both the smooth-muscle system and the neuronal system. A primary complaint of migraine headaches has led to a sense of helplessness, hopelessness and depression over the severe interruptions that migraine headaches cause in the person's private and professional lives.

In Figure 11, the very large circle represents the total activation of all systems, a catastrophic condition frequently associated with shock syndromes or complete nervous breakdowns. Constriction and inadequate arousal, indicated by the small inner circle, frequently develop as individuals pass into an almost vegetablelike comatose state.

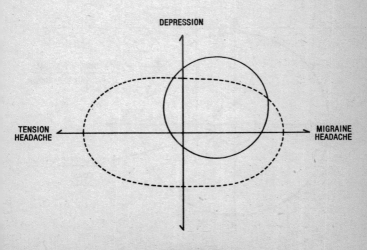

Figure 10

Which Path Will Overactivate?

What factors determine which of the compass points will become overactivated when a particular person experiences excessive stress? This question is still under study, but many researchers suspect that heredity and early life experiences influence individual vulnerability to particular types of illness. The question of a possible hereditary tendency to develop certain stress disorders is represented in Figure 12, in which the large arrow pointing to the right, toward smooth-muscle overactivation, represents a genetic tendency for this system in particular to be aroused when this person is experiencing stress and tension. Again symptoms could include migraine headaches, high blood pressure or asthma. Studies of identical twins are currently being conducted to clarify how stress activates these hereditary pathways.

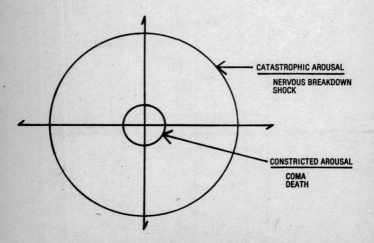

CATASTROPHIC AROUSAL
NERVOUS BREAKDOWN
SHOCK

CONSTRICTED AROUSAL
COMA
DEATH

Figure 11

In suggesting how early life experiences may predispose people to certain kinds of stress-related illness, the idea of the compass points of healthy and unhealthy stress complements Transactional Analysis, or TA, an analytic and therapeutic technique that is used by many psychologists. According to TA, which was developed by the late Dr. Eric Berne, each of us has within us a parent voice, an adult voice and a child voice, and within an unconscious system, one of these voices is directing our behavior at any given moment. If our conscience is bothering us, the parent is talking; if we're doing something silly and innocent and carefree, the child is speaking. Freud expressed similar concepts in terms of the id, ego and superego, and TA is an attempt to eliminate the Freudian jargon so that untrained people can understand these ideas.

The parent in each of us still acts on the child in each of us. The messages given to us as children by parents and authority figures are the sources of our parental voice: we internalize these messages and attempt to direct our lives according to them. The nature of the messages we have internalized has

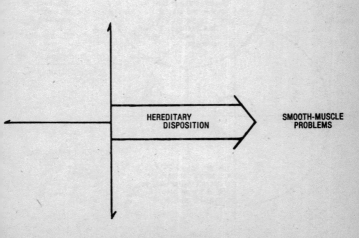

Figure 12

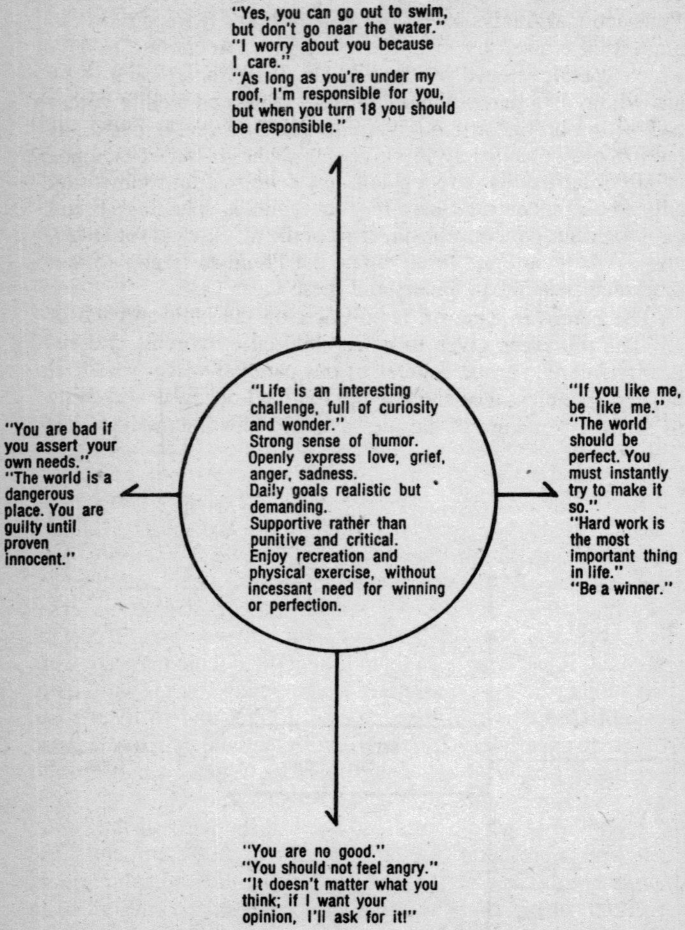

"Yes, you can go out to swim, but don't go near the water."
"I worry about you because I care."
"As long as you're under my roof, I'm responsible for you, but when you turn 18 you should be responsible."

"You are bad if you assert your own needs."
"The world is a dangerous place. You are guilty until proven innocent."

"Life is an interesting challenge, full of curiosity and wonder."
Strong sense of humor.
Openly express love, grief, anger, sadness.
Daily goals realistic but demanding.
Supportive rather than punitive and critical.
Enjoy recreation and physical exercise, without incessant need for winning or perfection.

"If you like me, be like me."
"The world should be perfect. You must instantly try to make it so."
"Hard work is the most important thing in life."
"Be a winner."

"You are no good."
"You should not feel angry."
"It doesn't matter what you think; if I want your opinion, I'll ask for it!"

Figure 13

a major influence on which of the compass-point mechanisms are most likely to be overactivated when we experience excessive stress. Figure 13 shows the kind of messages given by parents to children who tend to develop problems with each of the compass-point mechanisms.

Consider the messages grouped at the left of the figure. "You are bad if you assert your own needs," a mother tells her child. "The world is a dangerous place. You are guilty until proven innocent." Children exposed to such messages learn to expect great danger in the world outside. They walk through life like strangers in a tough neighborhood who expect to be robbed or assaulted at any moment. They tense their muscles in a protective posture, bracing against the perceived threat, ready to fight or flee. Parents thus program these children for chronic muscle tension, and the children become disposed for life to problems with the neuromuscular system, including cramps, low back pain and tension headache.

By contrast, consider the messages grouped at the top of the figure: "Yes, you can go out to swim, but don't go near the water"; "As long as you're under my roof I'm responsible for you, but when you turn eighteen you should be responsible." Such double messages are enormously stressful for people who have any tendency toward a major emotional disorder. Children exposed to them may later have trouble with the neuronal system and may develop emotional problems, ulcers, depression, neurotic illnesses, phobias, obsessive-compulsive patterns, psychotic episodes or schizophrenia. In the case of schizophrenia, it has long been thought that the double message from the mother is "I love you and I hate you." The growing child cannot predict which message she'll give, and so lives a life of great uncertainty that can lead to breakdown. (A genetic predisposition is probably also a factor.) We call a mother who gives such messages a *schizophrenigenic* mother.

Similarly, the messages grouped at the right of the figure can lead to problems with the smooth-muscle system, and those at the bottom can lead to hormonal difficulties. In comparison, the kind of messages and parental characteristics described in the circle can help children grow up to be relatively free of stress-related problems and to enjoy a balance of the four major body mechanisms.

The objective of the six-second QR technique is to train you to achieve a healthy balance of all four systems. The QR training exercises in Chapters 9 through 16 will help you to achieve increased regulation of awareness of stress (neuronal compass point), sensations of flowing heaviness (skeletal-muscle compass point) and flowing warmth (smooth-muscle and hormonal compass points). Thus the Quieting Reflex concept acts on components of all four mechanisms to achieve inner balance between an alert mind and a calm body with a capacity to "shift gears" to meet appropriately the stresses of daily life.

6. How QR Is Different

As the inadequacies of traditional medical approaches to stress-related diseases and the dangers of routine use of minor tranquilizers have been recognized in recent years, a variety of self-regulation techniques have been proposed as alternatives. Some of the procedures currently in widespread use include passive meditation, progressive relaxation, autogenic training, biofeedback training and "Open Focus." Each of these techniques has particular strengths and drawbacks, and QR is significantly different from all of them.

Passive Meditation

During the 1970s, after the potential health benefits of Transcendental Meditation became recognized, two secularized techniques derived from TM also came into widespread use. The first, developed by Dr. Herbert Benson, is called the Relaxation Response, and employs progressive muscle relaxation, quiet breathing and the repetition to oneself of the word "One." The second is Dr. Patricia Carrington's Clinically Standardized Meditation, which permits the beginning meditator to experiment and select his own mantra from a list of sixteen Sanskrit words. All three of these techniques are forms of passive meditation.

Although comparative studies to evaluate the relative merits of these similar procedures are currently under way, the TM organization has reportedly become reticent about exposing its technique to further scientific investigation. Its representatives have stated that so much scientific evidence supports the validity of TM that no more research needs to be done. But an objective examination of the scientific literature suggests that from about 1970 until 1975, research into TM yielded positive findings and the TM organization cooperated extensively with investigators. Then negative reports started coming out, and what began as a trickle grew into an avalanche.

Newer reports indicate that the effects of TM are not nearly as pronounced as had been reported originally. For example, in 1971, Keith Wallace, Ph.D., and Herbert Benson, M.D., published a paper in the *American Journal of Physiology* in which they reported that subjects showed as much as a 400 percent decrease in tension level, as indicated by measurements of galvanic skin resistance. Since then, no one outside the TM organization has reported a decrease of more than 30 percent.

Researchers have also shown that many experienced meditators, rather than defocusing their minds and keeping them blank by concentrating on their mantras, are in fact falling into a light stage of sleep. There have been reports that TM leads to an increased incidence of various types of headaches, and some physicians have begun to report cases of long-time meditators developing serious side effects characterized by very frightening experiences. According to these reports, someone who has meditated for too long at one time may experience what has been described as mental lightning—flashing light accompanied by pain shooting up the spine and into the head. This phenomenon, referred to as "northern lights" or "aurora borealis," is called *kundalini* energy in Yoga, and there is a whole school of Yoga devoted to developing it, but under guidance and within a spiritual framework, so that it doesn't cause negative symptoms. People trained in TM who meditate a lot and have this experience have not been taught how to deal with this "unstressing" side effect.

Confronted with more and more negative reports, along with failure to replicate the positive results of initial studies, it's possible that it seemed in the best interest of the TM organization to begin to discourage research by outside investigators. This stance is likely to encourage more widespread adoption of one of the derivative procedures.

But the major problem with all three passive meditation techniques is that people don't stick with them after they lose contact with their instructors or training groups. Transfer of training from the structured learning situation to the outside world is not effective. The passive meditation techniques require two twenty-minute practice periods a day in a quiet room, away from the stresses of life. They apparently work as long as one keeps practicing, but people soon stop taking the time to practice.

By comparison, QR is an active skill that can be used all day long at the "scene of the crime" of stressful events. It is compatible with all behaviors. Since it takes only six seconds, QR can be practiced as many as 60 to 100 times a day— whenever an annoyance or worry occurs—and still take less time than the passive meditation procedures. (Twenty minutes twice a day equals forty minutes; 6 seconds times 100 equals 600 seconds, or ten minutes total.) And rather than emphasize relaxation per se, QR provides a pause during which a person can decide whether a stress is an appropriate cause for arousing the body.

Why "Relaxation" Fails

Statistical data from around the country indicate low compliance for the passive meditation techniques: 10 percent for the Relaxation Response three months after the start of training, and slightly higher, 15 percent, for Clinically Standardized Meditation. TM has the highest compliance, probably because its mystique exerts a certain hold over its practitioners, but 30 percent at three months is still not very impressive.

In our work with various self-regulation techniques at the clinic, we tried to determine why potentially good programs like the Relaxation Response failed to regulate stress in our patients and why the interest and commitment of those in training dropped off after a brief period.

Our patients provided clear explanations. They felt they faced hundreds of tensions a day, ranging from financial pressures to problems with children to job difficulties to marital stresses. But their lives were very much a part of the Western life-style, demanding involvement, not withdrawal. A "dropout" activity like TM or Clinically Standardized Meditation, no matter how beneficial, was incompatible with their schedules. Practice became conditional upon convenience.

Patients were not motivated to do the twenty-minute morning practice after they had awakened from a restful night, because it seemed in conflict with the up-and-moving attitude that they brought to a new day. They were even less motivated to do the evening meditation, because of the practical demands of their home lives. They reported that they found it difficult to remove themselves from such family activities as helping with homework and providing companionship to their children and spouse. Evening is a natural time to become reinvolved with the family, rather than disengaged from them.

In contrast to the passive meditation techniques, QR clinics and patients reported an 80 percent or better compliance at two years! Why?

Patients indicated that they were willing to commit themselves to a six-second technique that did not require dropping out. They could do the sequence with their eyes open, at the moment of stress, while carrying on the commitment at hand. They controlled the technique; the technique didn't control them. In addition, the physiological approach that characterizes QR did not infringe on anyone's belief structure, as did the mystical elements of TM. And people were strongly motivated to persist in the QR because it felt good to do it.

Progressive Relaxation

Progressive relaxation, developed by Edmund Jacobson in the 1920s, helps people contrast the difference between extreme muscle tension and complete muscle relaxation, with the focus of the technique progressively moving from one region of the body to another. This practice permits finer and finer discrimination of the muscle tension states that lead to stress disorders. Progressive relaxation instructions are often used in conjunction with biofeedback instruments, and some contrasts between muscle tension and relaxation used in the QR training program are derived from Jacobson's technique.

Progressive relaxation can be very effective in enhancing health and minimizing problems such as tension headache, particularly when it is taught by a charismatic instructor over a period of many months. Most patients, however, view progressive relaxation as somewhat simplistic; the idea that progressively tensing and relaxing muscles could by itself lead to the alleviation of symptoms such as head pain is apparently outside the belief structure of most people. Nonetheless, progressive relaxation is an excellent way to develop awareness of muscle tension.

Autogenic Training

Autogenic training was developed in Europe by J. H. Schultz, a German, early in this century, and subsequently has been elaborately researched and popularized by Wolfgang Luthe. The technique uses postures, exercises and a set of self-suggestive phrases, such as "My hands are warm; my head is cool," to help individuals relieve symptoms by gaining voluntary control over various organ systems.

Unfortunately, optimal results with autogenic training require frequent contact with a highly trained practitioner. Because of the professional expense and the time necessary to achieve autogenic control of excessive stress responses, the technique has not been widely adopted as a "stand-alone" procedure in America, although portions of it are used in almost every software program devised to accompany biofeedback. Autogenic phrases, which generally emphasize feelings of heaviness and warmth in the body, are incorporated into the QR training program in a modified form.

Biofeedback

The principles of biofeedback, as well as the limitations—poor transfer out of the training situation and poor long-term compliance—have already been discussed. It should also be noted that biofeedback instruments used by themselves—without an instructional software program for relaxation or quieting—are seldom effective. This accounts for much disappointment with the technique on the part of individuals who have not been adequately trained. When biofeedback instruments are used by themselves, fewer than 10 percent of trainees continue to try to practice what they have learned after three months. While biofeedback must almost invariably be coupled with software procedures in order to be effective, the use of the QR program, as noted, makes the hardware of biofeedback—the instruments—unnecessary for about 80 percent of the people afflicted with the kinds of problems for which biofeedback is effective.

Open Focus

Open Focus, a relatively new method for self-regulation developed by Dr. Lester Fehmi, is presented as a series of exercises on audio cassettes. The technique is designed to produce an open, relaxed and integrated mind/body state in which focused awareness is diffused to include the totality of ongoing experience. In Open Focus, one develops a series of "objectless" mental pictures that facilitate the distribution of attention among various sensations in the body and various types of experience. A series of questions directed to the idea of spaces within the body, such as "Can you imagine the space, the distance, between your eyes?" stimulates the imagination of objectless experience. Open Focus produces a creative, "hand-loose" attitude that relieves compulsive tendencies such as writer's block—the tendency of a writer to want to get something down on paper so perfectly the first time that he becomes unable to begin at all.

Open Focus enables one to approach relaxation as effortlessly as possible. It can be contrasted with narrowly focusing the attention, which, because of the effort required to concentrate on one thing to the exclusion of others, can be counterproductive. The depth of relaxation that can be achieved with Open Focus is remarkable, but it is so profound that it can lead to what we call dissociative reactions, or feelings of unreality. Thus Open Focus is a powerful tool, but should only be used under the supervision of a highly qualified professional.

Open Focus techniques have not been incorporated into the QR training program. However, the QR technique entails both humor and flexibility of mental functioning, which similarly counteract the tendency to concentrate so intensely that the attentional process itself becomes stressful.

Quieting Any Time, Anywhere

Like the passive meditation techniques, virtually all the foregoing self-regulation procedures require fifteen to twenty minutes of practice twice daily in a quiet room away from stressful events, and thus present the same problem with compliance in practicing. Even if compliance with this schedule is good, QR, practiced throughout the day at the moment of stress, provides a superior ongoing quieting effect. Figure 14 attempts to demonstrate the differences among a typical Type A individual who increases his arousal level throughout the day, an individual doing QR for six seconds many times throughout the day to diffuse the potential buildup of arousal, and an individual using a self-regulation technique twice a day for fifteen to twenty minutes to control arousal. The figure makes clear the advantages of the quick technique that can be used any time and anywhere.

An Alert Mind and a Calm Body

Even more important, QR permits a person to maintain an alert Type A mind and a calm Type B body, with the ability to shift to a higher or lower level of arousal when circumstances demand.

Beginning with our early school experiences, most of us have been taught that the way to achieve in our complicated, high-pressure world is to try hard, harder and then harder still. This is the Western work ethic, which is remarkably effective in using our brains in what Friedman and Rosenman termed Type A behavior. The dilemma that creates a need for tranquilizers and techniques like QR is the misapplication of the Type A mental strategy and the Western work ethic to our bodies as well as our minds.

In Figure 15, the circle at left, indicating a Type A mind and a Type A body, represents a full arousal condition that is really appropriate only in athletic events or when we're faced with emergencies that threaten our physical well-being. Driven by the Western work ethic, we tend to maintain this Type A mind-Type A body condition, and this leads to the production of stress-related illnesses.

Tranquilizers and similar drugs create a new problem, in that their sedative action slows down both mental and physical activity, producing not only a Type B body, but a Type B mind, which is not competitive in our time-pressured society. The middle circle in Figure 15, representing the combination of a Type B mind and a Type B body, represents the state most people experience during sleep, as well as the state produced to a lesser degree by the use of minor tranquilizers.

A more desirable situation is indicated in the right-hand circle, in which a Type A mind compatible with our Western life-style is coupled with a Type B body that is not activated

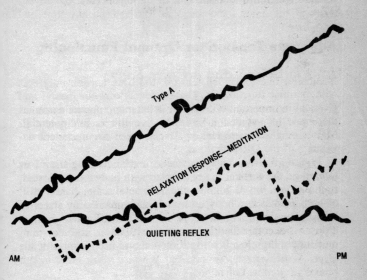

Figure 14

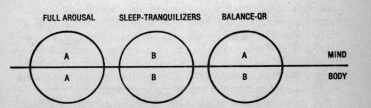

Figure 15

unless a true emergency is encountered. This is the state of balance fostered by the six-second QR technique.

Adequate Tension for Optimal Functioning

Ironically, like too much tension, too little tension interferes with optimal functioning. Certain levels of both mental and physical tension are necessary; it is the inappropriate extremes that must be avoided in order to live life at full potential. Maintaining adequate tension levels is another important advantage of the QR technique.

Figure 16 shows mental tension levels, running from low to high on the vertical scale, coupled with body tension levels, running from low to high on the horizontal scale. A low level of both mental and body tension is accompanied by states of lethargy or sleep, a state of low mental arousal and high body arousal is accompanied by nervous exhaustion, and a state of moderately high levels of both mental and body arousal tends

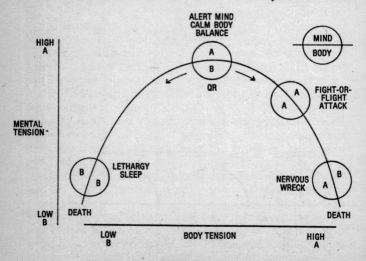

Figure 16

to be associated with relatively unthinking attack behaviors in which people, like cornered animals in a fight-or-flight situation, do not always consider alternatives. As this figure indicates, either too low or too high a level of body arousal is incompatible with life.

Again, the condition at the top of the curve, representing the balance of an alert mind and a calm body, is the state fostered by the QR skill. QR permits slight movement to the right or left on the curve in order to optimize mental functioning.

Inner Balance—Homeostasis

QR's goal, an inner balance that counters tendencies to arousal with mechanisms for quieting and recovery, is called *homeostasis* by scientists. It is achieved by two opposing parts of the nervous system—the parasympathetic, for low arousal or quieting functions, and the sympathetic, for high arousal and tension functions.

To maintain health, episodes of high arousal need to be balanced by periods of low arousal. The stress problems of modern man develop from the tendency to overactivate the sympathetic high-arousal system. This concept is illustrated in Figure 17, in which the solid line represents a state of shifting balance between high and low arousal, while the dotted line indicates a state in which the sympathetic high-arousal system is overactivated. So many people recognize at a commonsense level this tendency to overarouse that they assume that "downer" techniques should solve the problem. This accounts for the widespread popularity of tranquilizers and relaxation or meditation techniques. Unfortunately, as already mentioned, the "downer" techniques serve, in their one-dimensional emphasis, to merely flatten the curve, reducing the mental alertness possible at optimal balance.

QR permits an alert mind to shift into the best body "gear"— from "passing" to amused "coasting"—to deal with the stress at hand. It does not interfere with an emergency response when it is warranted. Indeed, because QR prevents the waste of energy through excessive stress responses to the pressures of ordinary living, one can react with more power and vigor to a real physical threat. Many coaches and athletes are already using QR for this purpose.

QR's emphasis on an alert mind that automatically shifts to an appropriate body gear encourages productive, active, constructive and positive behaviors, both mental and physical. The QR skill should not be confused with "so what" or "who-cares" techniques that encourage people to shrug off stress-producing situations; these techniques can produce negative personal and social behaviors. In fact, smiling with the eyes, which is part of the QR technique, improves social contact.

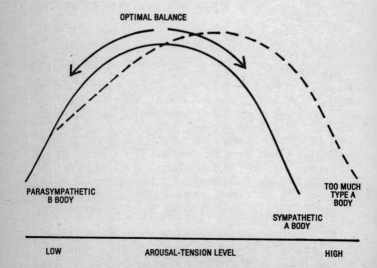

Figure 17

Shifting Gears to Meet the Stress of Life

The advantages of the QR "gear-shifting" technique are further illustrated by the case of Marion, the 38-year-old housewife who came to me complaining of migraine headaches that had afflicted her on the average of twice a month for the past twenty years and usually lasted about twenty-four hours. As already described, the mechanism of classic migraine headache is set in motion in susceptible people when the emergency response causes constriction of the arteries that carry blood to the brain and eyes. Invariably, about twenty minutes before Marion's headaches began she would see "little shooting stars"—doctors call them *scintillating scotomata*—and her vision would blur, both common symptoms believed to result from this blood vessel constriction. Then she would suffer a debilitating pulsating headache on one side of her head.

Marion was a superachiever who placed extremely high demands on herself. She belonged to many women's clubs, was supportive of her husband in his career, and tried to be all things to her three children. What set her apart from many migraine sufferers was that she never developed headaches while she was actually under stress, trying to cope with the demands of her daily home life or planning a party or getting ready for a vacation. Instead, once all her work was done—just as the party was about to begin, for example, or just as her family was about to climb in the car and head for their vacation spot—she would develop a headache so severe that the plans would have to be canceled. It was almost as if Marion had to stay busy to keep her headaches away. The migraine problem had disrupted her sexual relationship with her husband and had almost destroyed her family life. She and her husband had seen a family therapist but were nonetheless considering divorce.

By the time she came to the psychophysiology clinic, Marion had been through many medication regimens, but they had not been effective, and the drugs had produced unpleasant side effects. She was referred to the clinic for biofeedback and relaxation training, which are usually quite effective in relieving migraines. In Marion's case, however, after she'd been through the early biofeedback research program without QR instruction, her headaches actually became worse.

At that point, I realized that Marion needed to learn how to shift gears up or down to control her reactions to stress. Relaxation (as distinct from quieting) was actually the trigger that set off her headaches; the migraines always came "after the battle." We did need to teach her to quiet herself—to keep a calm Type B body in the face of daily pressures—but we also had to teach her that once the pressure was off, rather than collapsing completely, she needed to shift gears up to maintain some degree of tension.

I then introduced Marion to QR, without biofeedback. In the course of the training, she learned to distinguish where she was on the continuum from high to low arousal at any time, and to shift up a bit—to take on some level of activity or responsibility—when she found herself starting to go into the totally relaxed state that brought on her headaches. When her family was leaving by car on vacation, for example, she might get out a schedule, road maps, or other information about their trip and busy herself with plans. At the same time that she kept her mind active, the automatic QR would come into play if her body became overexcited—she would maintain a Type A mind and a Type B body.

After four months of practicing the six-second QR fifty to sixty times a day, Marion became headache free and has been so ever since. Her entire family is delighted and grateful, and they frequently send cards to us at the clinic saying that her cure has been the greatest miracle they could have hoped for.

When we offered Marion only the "downer" techniques of relaxation and biofeedback, we were unable to help her. In her case, the ability to shift up or down was essential to her self-cure.

Round-the-clock Self-regulation

Once the six-second Quieting Reflex becomes automatic through practice, it is triggered by a catch in the breathing rhythm. Studies are now under way at major sleep labs to determine whether it operates effectively during sleep, when a disturbing dream might cause an arousal reaction and thus an alteration in the breathing rhythm. Thus far the data are very promising. Should QR prove to be effective around the clock, as we believe it will, this will represent yet another crucial advantage over other self-regulation techniques.

Control of High Blood Pressure

Certain conditions for which self-regulation techniques are effective must be controlled twenty-four hours a day. Among them is essential, or unexplained, idiopathic hypertension—high blood pressure. Essential hypertension accounts for 90 percent of all high blood pressure cases; malignant hypertension, usually related to some problem with the kidneys, accounts for the remaining 10 percent.

Compliance in taking medication for high blood pressure is very low in this country. Only 11 percent of the people identified as having essential hypertension take the drugs that control it because the problem is usually a silent one, that is, it doesn't produce any discomfort. The medication, on the other hand, has a variety of negative side effects, including impotence, fatigue and depression, so people often stop taking it. Unfortunately, if essential hypertension is not controlled, it can lead to heart attack or stroke.

With biofeedback, people can learn quickly to regulate their blood pressure without medication, but while medication works when a person is asleep, there is no evidence that biofeedback training does. Should studies demonstrate that the automatic

Quieting Reflex does indeed operate even during the sleep state, it will represent an attractive alternative to medication for problems like essential hypertension.

We have already had considerable success in using QR to help hypertensive patients. Among them is Paul, a 44-year-old lawyer with a large criminal trial practice. Paul's hypertension was detected by his physician during his annual physical, and he was put on medication that brought his blood pressure under control but also rendered him impotent. Paul was enormously disturbed by the disruption of his sex life and began to seek a nonmedical way to control his blood pressure. His physician, who had read a paper on QR, referred him to me to learn the technique.

At first Paul had great difficulty with QR because he approached it with the same intensity with which he practiced law. He had to be reassured continually and reminded that he couldn't try too hard in doing a QR, that he had to be somewhat passive and *let* it happen to his body, rather than try to *make* it happen. He finally got the idea, however, and has been "normotensive"—has had normal blood pressure—for well over two years without medication.

Consistent with his driving personality. Paul, in his enthusiasm for QR, initially kept trying to give up his medication on his own, without checking with his physician. I finally had to tell him that unless he saw his doctor I would not continue to work with him. If you suffer from a condition that must be controlled by drugs, QR training may permit you to reduce or eliminate the medication, but the decision to do so *must be made by the prescribing physician, not by you personally*.

The data we have compiled on Paul show that his blood pressure is normal during the day when we measure it and when he measures it himself at night. I must emphasize again that the controlled studies seeking to determine QR's effectiveness during sleep are not yet complete, but whenever Paul wakes up and takes his blood pressure—and he usually awakens after a dream—it's always normal.

Sleep Deaths

The probable round-the-clock effectiveness of QR also suggests a possible solution to the problem of sleep apnea, a sudden-death syndrome that mostly affects adult males and has been documented as the cause of 1500 deaths per year. The normal impulse to breathe, which is based on a buildup of carbon dioxide in the blood, apparently is lost during sleep in a certain percentage of men. Sufferers tend to be such heavy snorers that they keep their partners awake most of the night. As the partner lies awake, however, the man's snoring suddenly stops and he doesn't breathe for a minute and a half to two minutes. Naturally, the alarmed woman awakens her mate and often insists that he see a doctor. The diagnosis of sleep apnea is usually made from this kind of history. The current approach to this syndrome calls for the man to wear an alarm system every night, but if he forgets to wear the alarm or sleeps alone, he may die.

Because a catch, or holding, in the breathing pattern becomes the substitute cue as the Quieting Response becomes the Quieting Reflex, the implication of our ongoing research is that QR may be a treatment for this condition. After six months of developing an automatic QR, the patient would be protected, because when he stopped breathing, a whole new set of mechanisms, other than the buildup of carbon dioxide, would trigger the Quieting Reflex—and breathing is an integral part of the Quieting Reflex. The potential is exciting, especially since the actual number of deaths from sleep apnea is probably several times higher than the documented 1500 cases per year.

A Self-reinforcing Technique

Brevity, automaticity, high long-term compliance and the maintenance of an alert mind and a calm body with the capacity to shift arousal "gears" all make QR a superbly effective self-regulation technique. In addition, QR does not require many hours of expensive training by a therapist; it can be learned from this book. QR is not a potpourri of scattered "stress-management" techniques nor a pie-in-the-sky holistic health overview, nor does it depend on the mystique characteristic of meditation. Rather, it is grounded on sound physiological principles, including the learning-curve concept, the idea of practicing at the very moments when stress stimuli are present, and the fact that it is incompatible with the physiology of the first six seconds of the emergency response. Even at the early stages of learning, QR is self-reinforcing, because the physiological sensations of the QR steps feel good, and the technique produces notable results quickly.

7. Charting Your Stress Problem

An important function of a coach or teacher who is helping an athlete, singer, speaker—or overly tense person—develop a new skill is detection of behavioral patterns that obstruct learning. In chapter 2, I described using our family picture album to discover facial tension and unusual body postures that indicated such patterns in myself. Similarly, many coaches advise students to practice in front of a mirror, or use movies or video tapes of practices and competitions as diagnostic aids. After all, until some sort of evaluation has been made, the learner doesn't really know what needs to be corrected.

How Do You Rate Yourself?

Because a personal coach will not be available for people using this book to learn the QR technique, I have developed rating

charts and the QR Diary Scan to help you heighten your awareness of stress and tension and help you chart your progress and
maintain your commitment to the QR training program. They
will also allow you to recognize mental and physical states that
may be slowing your learning.

Many of us develop signs of tension, restlessness, uneasiness or annoyance without a clear idea of the source of these
problems. Differentiating between mental tension and body
tension is a first and clarifying step. As I've already suggested,
a good example of mental tension is lying in bed trying to
sleep, with a body that feels physically tired but a mind that
is restless and won't stop thinking or going over the day's
events. Other symptoms of mental tension are listed in the
rating scale below. Take a moment now to rate the incidence
of these symptoms in your life. A score of more than 10 suggests that you are experiencing problems from mental tension.

Symptoms of Mental Tension

Rating

_____	Feeling anxious, tense, irritable or isolated
_____	Social fears
_____	Fears of heights, or darkness, or of being alone
_____	Low self-esteem
_____	Sexual worries
_____	Generalized anxiety without apparent cause
_____	Eating too much or too little
_____	Sleeping difficulties
_____	Time too slow or fast
_____	Accidentals (see page 124)
_____	**Total**

Rating points: 0 = never, 1 = sometimes, 2 = frequently

As an example of body tension, recall nights when your mind
was extremely fatigued from the day's activities, but your body
was restless and you were unable to find a position in bed that
would permit you to fall asleep. Following is a body tension
rating scale that can help you evaluate your incidence of body
tension. A problem is indicated by a score of more than 20.

Symptoms of Body Tension

Rating   *Cardiovascular*
_____   Palpitations
_____   Racing heart ("so fast I could die")
_____   Dizziness
_____   Faintness
_____   Fear of loss of consciousness
_____   Blushing
_____   Fainting
_____   Migraine headaches
_____   Cold hands or feet

              Respiratory
_____   Unable to get enough air into lungs
_____   Hyperventilation (shallow, fast breathing)
_____   Chest constriction, oppression or pain

              Muscular
_____   Tension headaches
_____   Tremor
_____   Shaking
_____   Severe weakness
_____   Restless body or legs
_____   Jaw grinding

              Gastrointestinal
_____   Butterflies in stomach
_____   Nausea
_____   Vomiting
_____   Flatulence (gas, burping)
_____   Discomfort, fullness
_____   Abdominal pain, cramps

              Other
_____   Sweating
_____   Pimples
_____   **Total**

Rating points: 0 = never, 1 = sometimes, 2 = frequently

Ironically, a score below 5 on the mental tension checklist or
below 10 on the body tension checklist suggests that you may

not be tense *enough* for optimal functioning. As already noted, certain levels of both mental and physical tension are necessary for productive and creative functioning.

The QR Diary Scan

As you proceed with the QR training, you will use the QR Diary Scan on pages 126–27 each day. On a scale from high to low, you will rate seven general factors that either affect or reflect states of mental or body tension. The factors rated on the QR Diary Scan are as follows:

Environmental pressures. This category covers influences beyond your control, including weather, traffic, poor sleep conditions or work pressures imposed on you from without. If these or similar pressures play a major intrusive role in your life on a given day, you will rate environmental pressures as high.

Annoyances/Accidentals. This category covers a short temper, any tendency for little things to get on your nerves, and "accidentals"—my word for little accidents like minor cuts or bumps, lapses of memory or slips of the tongue. If you experience an increased incidence of annoyances or accidentals, your rating for that day is high.

Time Pressures. Your sense of time pressure may be low or high on a given day. If you feel way behind in your schedule, the rating for time pressure is high.

Emotional Frustrations. Each day you will ask yourself whether feelings interfered with your ability to think clearly and whether you've overreacted or underreacted to situations, then rate yourself accordingly.

Fatigue. Difficulty in sleeping the previous night, trouble in remaining alert during the day, or a hangover or illness all warrant a high fatigue rating.

Body Tension. If scanning your body reveals excessive bracing or muscle tension, or if you've been unusually fidgety or experienced unexplained muscle twitches, your body tension rating will be high.

QR Diary Scan

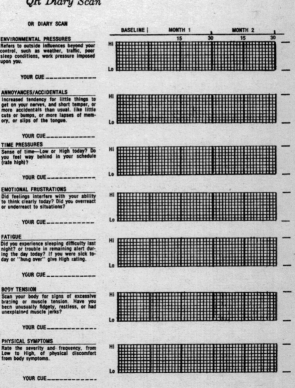

QR DIARY SCAN

ENVIRONMENTAL PRESSURES
Refers to outside influences beyond your control, such as weather, traffic, poor sleep conditions, work pressure imposed upon you.

YOUR CUE _____

ANNOYANCES/ACCIDENTALS
Increased tendency for little things to get on your nerves, and short temper, or more accidentals than usual. like little cuts or bumps, or more lapses of memory, or slips of the tongue.

YOUR CUE _____

TIME PRESSURES
Sense of time—Low or High today? Do you feel way behind in your schedule (rate high)?

YOUR CUE _____

EMOTIONAL FRUSTRATIONS
Did feelings interfere with your ability to think clearly today? Did you overreact or underreact to situations?

YOUR CUE _____

FATIGUE
Did you experience sleeping difficulty last night? or trouble in remaining alert during the day today? if you were sick today or "hung over" give High rating.

YOUR CUE _____

BODY TENSION
Scan your body for signs of excessive bracing or muscle tension. Have you been unusually fidgety, restless, or had unexplained muscle jerks?

YOUR CUE _____

PHYSICAL SYMPTOMS
Rate the severity and frequency, from Low to High, of physical discomfort from body symptoms.

YOUR CUE _____

BASELINE | MONTH 1   MONTH 2
        15   30   15   30

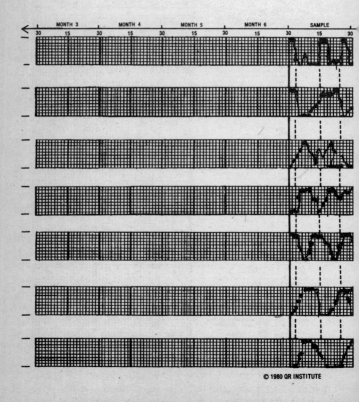

Physical Symptoms. This category covers the severity and frequency of your physical discomforts.

The graphs for rating yourself on each of these factors each day extend out to the right from these headings on the QR Diary Scan. They cover a baseline period, for evaluation before you begin to acquire the QR skill, and then a period of six months, the usual interval required to develop automaticity. At the far right of the graphs, a sample section shows how the daily ratings are made for each of the seven factors. (For months that have thirty-one days, you can combine ratings for two days; for shorter months, leave one or two sets of rating squares blank.)

The environmental events, feelings and body states that the QR Diary Scan asks you to review are easily remembered on the day they occur, but are quickly forgotten with the pressures of successive busy days. Rhythms or trends producing distress, which previously may have escaped your attention, are easily detected by the Diary Scan.

After you've filled out the Diary Scan for several weeks, you can slide a ruler across the page vertically to see if any peaks occurring in the first six factors correlate with the seventh factor—physical symptoms. (In the sample section, the dotted lines indicate such correlations.) This practice will help you better understand how environmental pressures, annoyances, time pressures, emotional frustrations and body tension affect your experience of physical symptoms.

By encouraging you to examine your moods, emotions and physical states in seven major areas of functioning each day, the QR Diary Scan heightens your awareness of how mental events affect your body and bodily events affect your mental functioning. In addition, it provides a record of your progress. A runner trying to increase his or her capacity to jog a long distance usually likes to keep some kind of graphic record of improvements and setbacks over the course of training. The QR Diary Scan serves a similar function in the QR training.

Most people who are trying to lose weight, quit smoking or drinking, or reduce anxiety are attempting to reverse habits that have been acquired through many months, if not years, of practice. Regrettably, it has been my experience that they frequently find convenient excuses to stop the very practice that will help them achieve new self-mastery and control over the function in question. To avoid this pitfall and help you carry out the QR training, you will find it useful to place a bookmark at the pages devoted to the QR Diary Scan and keep the book available by your bedside or carry it with you. This will serve as a reminder to make ratings on the seven factors every single day for the next six months, not only to increase your awareness of emotions, moods and physical symptoms that seem to go together, but to reinforce your practicing behavior.

Start rating yourself on the seven Diary Scan factors today. Ideally, to develop an accurate "baseline," you should rate yourself for the next two weeks before beginning the exercises in Session 1 of the QR Training, which comprise chapter 9. If you are eager to proceed with the QR training without waiting two weeks, you can, as an alternative, construct a baseline by reviewing the last two weeks. As noted, however, detailed memory of these states is notoriously poor.

Make a Contract for Health

"Contracting" is an additional technique that helps many people stick with a practice schedule aimed at changing behavior. Now, while you are most enthusiastic about acquiring the six-second QR technique as a way to eliminate the negative effects of stress from your life, I strongly urge you to read Contract With Myself, on page 130. Fill in the blanks according to the instructions, which follow, and sign it, as a firm commitment to yourself that you will pursue all of the QR instructions over the next six months.

The second clause of the contract calls for you to familiarize yourself with the medical precautions that apply to the QR training program and consult your physician if appropriate. QR is a powerful technique, and if you are already under treatment by a professional for a medical or psychological problem, it is mandatory that you discuss the contents of this book with him or her before you proceed with the training program. This is especially true if you are on medication for a condition such as epilepsy, low thyroid function, asthma, high blood pressure or diabetes that requires insulin injections. Have him or her review the list of problems on pages 106–107.

Caution is needed because as QR skills become relatively automatic, you will experience fewer excessive stress responses, which may in turn lead to a reduced need for many medications that become more effective when fewer stress hormones, such as adrenaline, are in the bloodstream. Although this is a desirable result, the decision to change medication levels must be made by the prescribing physician, and not by you personally. Medications such as those for high blood pressure function in your body twenty-four hours a day. Until QR works in a similar fashion, you can protect yourself from excessive stress responses only during the waking state, when you are actively practicing the QR.

Contract With Myself

I am about to undertake a personal learning program called Quieting Reflex Training (QR).

While I understand that QR is a learned skill and not a medical treatment, I have carefully read the medical precautions and have consulted my physician about any precautions that apply to me. I will consult my physician immediately if I sense any symptoms.

I assume full responsibility for the specified practicing schedule which is crucial if the QR is to become an automatic life skill.

I am committed to daily completion of my QR Diary Scan for the next six months.

I am committed to following the schedules and sequence of instructions specified in my QR text.

_____has agreed to go over my forms and talk with me about QR at least every two weeks over the next six months to serve as an objective observer who may notice things that I don't.

I set the following penalty for myself if I should fail to abide by this contract:

I set the following reward for myself when I complete the six-month QR training program successfully:

Signed_____

Observer_____

Date_____

The painstaking research carried out by the developer of autogenic training, Dr. Wolfgang Luthe, and his colleagues, has established an extensive data base of proper and improper applications that probably pertain to all forms of self-regulation training, including QR. If you have been diagnosed as having any of the following problems, the QR training may still be undertaken, but you will need the supervision of a trained professional who understands how a reduction in excessive arousal and stress responses will affect your condition.

1. You have a feeling of helplessness or hopelessness, depression or any sort of suicidal thought.

2. You've been told that you have a psychotic condition, or members of your family or a professional have told you that you are having difficulty maintaining contact with reality.

3. Your physician has told you that you suffer from a significant degree of arteriosclerosis, or hardening of the arteries.

4. You have suffered a stroke or have a history of frequent fainting spells.

5. You suffer from a constant or progressive headache problem.

6. Friends, family members or business associates frequently tell you that you have trouble following directions.

7. You suffer from some form of diabetes, particularly those forms requiring daily insulin injections.

8. You've been diagnosed as having a thyroid condition and are taking thyroid medication.

9. You've been diagnosed as having high blood pressure and are taking medication for the condition. (If you have been

diagnosed as having high blood pressure but are not taking medication, you should see your physician immediately to consider such medication, monitored through a series of appointments while you undertake QR training under supervision.)

10. You suffer from a convulsive disorder such as epilepsy.

11. You are taking minor tranquilizers. (You should recognize that your training period may be as long as eight to twelve months because the tranquilizer is interrupting and dampening the stress pathways that QR teaches you to regulate.)

There are now professionals familiar with the QR technique and its implications in almost all the major population centers in this country. The Biofeedback Society of America (4301 Owens Street, Wheat Ridge, CO 80033) publishes a list of individuals certified as competent in self-regulation techniques—not only biofeedback, but many of the adjunct techniques, including QR.

An Objective Observer

The sixth clause of the QR Contract With Myself contains a blank space for the name of a person whom you see on a regular basis, preferably daily, who will agree to go over your Diary Scan with you at least every two weeks and talk with you about your experiences as you become increasingly accomplished in the QR technique. This objective outsider may be able to make the helpful observations that a personal coach or teacher would make.

The next clause suggests setting a penalty for yourself in the event that you fail to pursue your goals in acquiring the QR skill. For many people, this penalty principle can be served by writing out five or six checks for a modest but painful sum, which you will send off one by one to your least favorite charities if you are failing to comply with the overall training program. It is a good idea to give these checks to your observer-colleague for safekeeping and disbursement should your biweekly discussions reveal that you've begun to slip in your practicing.

The final clause of the contract with yourself calls for rewarding yourself with something you really want once you've completed the entire six-month training program as specified in this book. If you've been longing for a piece of stereo equipment that's just beyond your family's means, you may want to sit down with your family and say, "I've signed this contract with myself to do the QR technique, and we're going to start putting away a certain amount each month so that I can get this piece of stereo equipment if I complete the QR program in six months." If you've got your eye on a special piece of clothing, you may want to put it on lay-away pending the completion of your training. This clause is a provision for indulging yourself a bit with something that you've wanted but would feel guilty about buying under other circumstances. Along with the Diary Scan, the QR Contract With Myself is a key element in helping you persist in learning and gaining automaticity in the QR skill that can do so much to enhance the quality of your life in more substantial ways.

8. Introduction to the QR Training Exercises

Before you proceed with the experiential learning exercises of the QR training, presented in chapters 9 through 16, you should become familiar with the important QR concepts discussed in the following pages. If these ideas seem difficult to grasp now, their meaning will unfold vividly when you experience the various aspects of the QR training.

The following lists contrast the initial six seconds of the emergency response with the competing hierarchy that comprises the six-second QR technique. During the training exercises, you will experience the exact meaning of each of the components of the six-second Quieting Reflex.

Initial Phases of
Emergency Response (Six Seconds)

1. Sympathetic nervous system activation; paying close attention to perceived threat
2. Tensing of muscles, especially facial muscles
3. Catching or holding breath or panting
4. Clenching jaws; constriction of blood flow to hands and feet

Contrary Phases of
Quieting Response (Six Seconds)

1. Cue: Tension, annoyance, anxiety, alteration in breathing
     Response:
2. Smile inwardly and with eyes and mouth
     Self-suggestion: "Alert amused mind, calm body."
3. Easy deep breath
4. While exhaling breath, let jaw, tongue and shoulders go limp; feel wave of heaviness; feel warmth flowing through body to toes
     Resume normal activity

Figure 18 contrasts the elements of the emergency response and the QR, showing how each QR element is incompatible with the corresponding emergency response element. The dotted lines indicate how, with practice, substitution of cues takes place, so that while the cue for a Quieting *Response* is a fear, threat or worry, the cue for the Quieting *Reflex* is a catch or other alteration in the breathing rhythm.

The QR Pyramid

The first session of the QR training exercises will introduce you to the basic six-second technique. This session will teach you how to be more aware of signs of tension and stress in your body. The pyramid in Figure 19 indicates the sequential levels that you will encounter as you explore each aspect of the QR technique in subsequent sessions. First you will carry out exercises in breathing, then learn to develop sensations of flowing heaviness by quieting your skeletal muscles, and then learn to develop sensations of flowing warmth by quieting your smooth muscles. When these levels are at last brought together, your QR will be a six-second mental pause occurring when you face stress, that will facilitate the use of humor, flexibility and mental imagery to "gearshift" the lower functions of the pyramid to suit the situation.

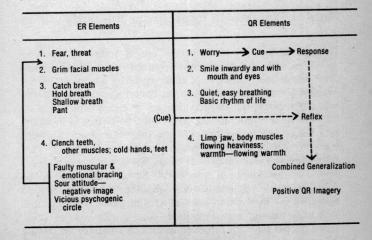

Figure 18

Quieting Response Training—Six Months

I like the image of a pyramid because the goal of the QR training is to establish a sound, grounded structure, in which the body is not driving the observing mind. The pyramid embodies some kind of latent symbolism that has been with the human race for thousands of years. The Egyptians were fascinated by it, and many traditions since have utilized the image of a pyramid with an all-seeing eye at the top. In fact, you can find one on the back of any American dollar bill.

The pyramid can also be seen to represent the learning curve by which you will acquire the QR skill. Your learning will start slowly, at the broad base of the pyramid, with the relatively long exercises in the following chapters. With practice, you will become more and more proficient, until you achieve the automatic six-second Quieting Reflex—the peak of the pyramid.

Mental Pictures to Reprogram the Body

Throughout the QR training, the use of imagery—creating mental pictures—is an essential element in producing the desired sensations. This use of imagery takes advantage of the fact that some area of the brain has communication with every cell in the body; the imagery is used to create a mental state that will help reprogram the part of the body that is involved in a faulty bracing effort or some other unconscious faulty reaction. An emerging theory called Neuro Linguistic Programming suggests that each of us has a particular style of perceptual awareness of our world. Some people tend to be *visualizers*—they remember best what they see. Some tend to be *auditory*—they remember best what they hear. Other people have to go through actual motions—they are *kinesthetic* types. Some people have all three tendencies in combination. In the QR program, we deal with all three tendencies, using visual, auditory and kinesthetic imagery.

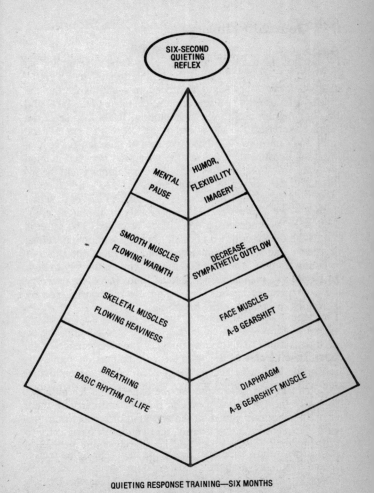

QUIETING RESPONSE TRAINING—SIX MONTHS

Figure 19

A–B Gearshift Muscles

To produce the desired state of an alert Type A mind and an efficient, low-arousal, Type B body able to shift to a Type A state when necessary, the QR procedure—and hence the exercises—focuses on two sets of muscles: those of the face, and the diaphragm muscle used in breathing. In the course of the training exercises, the sensations of the QR will be generalized to all body muscles, but these two sets of muscles get special emphasis because they are unique gearshifts between manual and automatic functioning—between the voluntary and the involuntary, the conscious and the unconscious. While we can contort our facial muscles at will—to make a face, or to scowl or blink—we also use them unconsciously in displaying emotions or as we undergo an emergency response. The same is true of the diaphragm: we normally breathe without conscious awareness, but we can voluntarily hold our breath or alter our breathing rhythm. The face and diaphragm are the key to how QR begins as a manual response to an annoyance, fear or worry and with practice becomes an automatic reflex triggered by alterations in regular, quiet breathing.

How to Practice

The chapters that follow present the experiential learning exercises of the QR training. When reading and carrying them out, remember that you're not in any kind of competition, not out to set records or win awards, and you don't have to try to do better than anyone else. You are simply going to learn a new skill that will improve your ability to function in a pressured society and enhance your life-style.

Take your time reading the exercises, going back over any material you feel you do not understand at first. Repeat the exercises as often as you feel you need to. You may find yourself puzzled by occasional instructions to wiggle your toes and fingers. This is a simple technique to arouse you—to help you shift gears up—when you may be slipping into reverie at the end of a long exercise. There are also occasional instructions to close your eyes when performing an exercise. If the instruction to close your eyes is not given, but you want to do so, go ahead. Closing your eyes simply helps you focus on the step or image you're working on.

You don't have to learn everything exactly, as long as you get a basic understanding of what each section is about. When you are instructed to repeat phrases or sentences, you don't have to repeat them word for word; use whatever phrases or words work for you.

Sit in a comfortable chair in a quiet room while you read and practice the exercises. Do not lie down, as you may tend to fall asleep if you do.

As already described, the QR exercises are divided into eight learning sessions, and while the six-second technique is introduced in Session 1 and should be used thereafter whenever you encounter an annoyance, remember that it takes most adults between four and six months of practice to develop automaticity.

The recommended learning sequence is as follows:

1. Read Session 1 (chapter 9) now. Do not proceed to Session 2 (chapter 10) until you feel comfortable and thoroughly familiar with Session 1 and have begun to consciously use the six-second Quieting Response when you encounter annoyances.

2. From the time you read Session 1, begin practicing the six-second Quieting Response throughout each day when you encounter annoyances—this may be as many as 50 to 100 times a day. Rate yourself on the seven graphs of the QR Diary Scan every day.

3. Schedule a time about five days from now when you will read and practice Session 2. Continue practicing the six-second Quieting Response throughout each day.

4. Schedule the remaining six sessions at five- to seven-day intervals. Going through all the sessions at one sitting *is*

not productive and can be confusing. Thousands of papers in psychological literature indicate that such "mass practice"—cramming for a test is an example—results in poorer learning than studying steadily over a longer period.

5. As mentioned, the exercises should be practiced in a sitting position. After you've completed Session 6, however, you should perform the QR Bedtime Daily Review Exercise, which concludes that session, each night while you lie in bed ready to fall asleep. It is almost a universal experience of the people who "get" QR—the 80 percent who achieve automaticity—that if they do QR while lying flat on their backs in bed with the intention of going to sleep, they fall asleep within fifteen or twenty seconds. Except in depressed people, insomnia is one of the conditions most responsive to QR. After you've learned the technique, you'll find that if something particularly unsettling has occurred during the day, using this longer exercise will induce sleep very rapidly.

Behaviors to Watch For

As people acquire the QR skills, they begin to experience fewer excessive stress responses and a general lowering of the level of arousal to which they have become accustomed. Even though people who normally function with a Type A mind and a Type A body often experience physical discomfort from overarousal of their stress mechanisms, they may feel uneasy when they achieve competence in QR and reduce their body discomfort. They have become so used to their migraine headaches or tension headaches or to taking pills for high blood pressure that they begin to feel uncomfortable when this set of behaviors—which has previously occupied so much of their time and frequently dominated their conversations—is eliminated. They feel a new uneasiness, a sense that something is not right. Should you experience such uneasiness, you should be aware of several negative patterns that perhaps 10 percent of the people who learn QR develop as they become proficient in the six-second technique.

Sometimes, when the most predominant symptom that an

individual has been experiencing begins to become less of a problem, he begins to focus on a secondary symptom that he previously ignored and to develop new concerns about what before might have been called suppressed symptoms.

Other people "trade" the symptom that has influenced their life-style so much for some form of maladaptive behavior. They may become depressed, or become so compulsively concerned about practicing QR that there's little time for other activity. Or they may see their new-found freedom as an occasion to "act out," becoming reckless in driving or other activities from which they previously had to abstain for fear of aggravating their symptom.

A third pattern, "scapegoating," is a focusing of attention on a significant other person, usually within the family unit, whose problems have previously been ignored. For example, a mother of small children, who once suffered from frequent migraine headaches but has become headache free through QR, may develop excessive concern about why little Johnny isn't doing better in school.

Many people eliminate such maladaptive behaviors just by becoming aware of them. If you find you're adopting one of these patterns, the first thing to do is talk it over with the outside observer you designated in your contract with yourself in chapter 7, page 105. Then decide whether you should seek professional advice about the next steps to take. If you find that you can't reverse this new behavior by yourself through awareness, you may want to talk with your family physician or with a psychiatrist or other certified professional.

Smug Self-mastery

I have also observed that as people who are learning the QR technique achieve automaticity, some develop a kind of smugness, almost as if they are laughing at people who haven't been exposed to QR. Family members who don't know a person is going through the program may begin to ask, "How come you're different? Why don't you get rattled the way you used to? Why don't you scream and tear your hair and have fits?"

And many QR trainees won't tell anybody that they've learned a mental exercise that has changed the way life's stresses affect them.

This smugness is founded on a good feeling—it develops as people begin to experience self-mastery and realize that they are no longer at the mercy of a passing-gear body. Symptoms and problems are disappearing and they feel more in control of their lives. But when asked about their new calm demeanor, they often just smile like Buddhas. We've had family members actually come to the clinic to find out what has changed their relatives' behavior so dramatically, and many have then gone through QR training themselves. I can't call this smugness a maladaptive behavior—it's more a reflection of human nature and of the competitive society in which we live. Certainly an automobile salesman who believes QR has given him an edge by relieving the anxiety he feels when dealing with customers may not be eager to tell other salesmen what he's learned. But naturally I'd prefer that people whose lives have been changed for the better by QR would share their experiences with others.

Reversing a Lifetime Habit

You are now ready to begin the QR training exercises. Because the Quieting Reflex is a new skill, quite different from anything you've done before, learning it will take time and practice. The tendencies acquired over a lifetime cannot be reversed overnight, and most of us have spent a lifetime acquiring a Type A mind-Type A body state. So settle yourself comfortably now and continue reading.

9. Session 1: Introducing the QR Technique

As previous chapters have explained, the Quieting Reflex is a brief contrary response to inappropriate gearing of the body to fight or flight. It begins in the early training phases as a consciously practiced Quieting Response, a set of behaviors that are exactly opposed to those of the emergency response, to things that get on our nerves, annoy us, frustrate or anger us. The two responses cannot occur together, and with repetition the Quieting Response becomes a virtually automatic Quieting Reflex. By learning the Quieting Reflex, we produce a new adaptive state in which we don't allow our bodies to become aroused when it is not appropriate.

Achieving automaticity in the six-second Quieting Reflex is the ultimate goal of the QR training. It is important to keep this goal in mind during the progressive training program, in which each exercise and image gradually and sequentially builds the component skills that culminate in the QR itself. These skills build like the levels of a pyramid to the automatic QR. The initial training exercises—the broad base of the pyramid—require about twenty-five minutes each. The resulting Quieting Reflex—the peak of the pyramid—requires only six seconds.

The steps of the QR toward which you are working are as follows:

Step One: A Cue—Awareness of a Worry, Annoyance or Anxiety.

Many of us become so accustomed to the presence of stress and tension in our lives that we lose the ability to discriminate between events that should call forth the emergency response and those for which such a response is inappropriate. Daily use of the QR Diary Scan will help you develop awareness of this.

Try Step One now. Become aware of a cue, that is, of a worry, annoyance or anxiety. If you're not aware of such a cue, thrust your tongue against the top of your mouth for several seconds until it becomes painful, in order to create an awareness of tension.

Step Two: Smile Inwardly With Your Mouth and Eyes, and Say to Yourself, "Alert Mind, Calm Body."

We all feel good when we are happy. This step and its supporting training elements attempt to promote a quiet sense of amusement and distance when we might otherwise let our bodies get out of control. The smile promotes loosening of the facial muscles around the mouth and eyes, relieving the grim set of the facial muscles that characterizes tension. By coupling the simple exercises of alert smiling with the self-suggestion that one's body muscles can be calm, relief from grim muscle tension in the face is generalized to all body muscles.

Repeat Step Two now. Smile inwardly with your mouth and eyes, and say to yourself, "Alert mind, calm body." Then repeat this step once more, just because it's pleasant to do.

Step Three: Inhale an Easy, Natural Breath

Breathing is the basic rhythm of life, and if regular and easy, has a profound calming influence on the body. This has been experienced by many people who have taken part in yoga programs. In contrast to those often lengthy and complex procedures, however, QR utilizes a single easy breath, inhaled and exhaled, along with imagery to evoke sensations that are part of more extensive breathing training programs. One QR training exercise will involve placing your hand against your chest or abdomen while passively paying attention as you breathe in and out at a comfortable pace; this will help you contrast anxious, uncomfortable breathing with quiet, gentle, normal breathing. Another exercise will combine calm breathing with a sensation of flowing warmth; placing the palm of one hand in front of your slightly parted lips, you will notice the warmth of your breath and a pleasant inward feeling of control as you discover and regulate your breathing patterns. The object of these exercises is to develop your awareness that certain breathing patterns are a sign of tension and to recognize that you have the power to modulate your breathing to a comfortable pace suitable for the task before you.

Repeat Step Three now. Inhale an easy, natural breath, while mentally counting *one, two, three*. Now exhale, counting *one, two, three*.

Step Four: While Exhaling, Let Your Jaw, Tongue and Shouders Go Loose. Feel a Wave of Limpness, Heaviness and Warmth Flowing to Your Toes as You Let Your Breath Out.

Try Step Four now: Inhale: *one, two, three*. Now exhale, letting your jaw, tongue and shoulders go loose, feeling a wave of limpness, heaviness and warmth flowing to your toes.

This step has a number of objectives, among them releasing

the muscle tension of clenched teeth, a thrusting tongue or tense shoulder and neck muscles. Feeling a wave of limpness, which most people experience almost immediately when they let their jaws drop, closely duplicates the sensation of flowing warmth and heaviness reported by individuals learning quieting while attached to biofeedback instruments. Many of the body awareness exercises in the QR program will help you experience these sensations.

One procedure involves gently placing your fingertips on your jaw joints just in front of your ears. Do this now. With your fingertips in place, open and close your mouth several times, noticing the movement of your jawbone where it connects to your skull. Observe the changes in your body sensations and the feeling of your jaw muscles as you inhale, then exhale and let your jaw go loose.

You can also experiment with the pleasant sensation of jaw looseness by parting your lips slightly, placing one set of fingers on your chin and gently manipulating your jaw into a comfortable position. The facial muscles, used in chewing, talking and unconsciously expressing anxiety and stress, are powerful, and it is remarkable how much you can relieve the tension in them.

Learning QR is pleasurable and fun. One exercise, while combining jaw limpness with breathing exercises, will introduce the idea of imaginary breathing pores in your feet. The image of air moving inside your body, combined with the apparently simple act of letting go of the jaw muscles, will produce sensations of flowing heaviness and warmth.

Try Step Four again to see if you can feel the limpness from your "jaw drop" extending into a sensation of flowing heaviness and warmth throughout your body and legs as you exhale. Review the instructions for Step Four first, then close your eyes and practice until you feel comfortable doing it. Open your eyes and continue reading.

Resume normal activity.

QR is entirely compatible with all ongoing daily life experiences. Performed at the very moment of stress, it helps foster the state of an alert mind in a calm, quiet body. It does not involve dropping out, becoming inattentive or getting out of touch with daily activity. As you become proficient in doing the QR relatively automatically, you will be amazed at your new positive, creative focus in many aspects of your life.

Let's conclude this session by doing a QR:

First, become aware of an annoyance, worry or anxiety. If you don't sense one now, create tension by thrusting your tongue against the roof of your mouth for several seconds.

Second, smile inwardly with your mouth and eyes, and say to yourself, "Alert mind, calm body."

Third, inhale an easy, natural breath.

Fourth, while exhaling, let your jaw, tongue and shoulders go loose, feeling a wave of limpness, heaviness and warmth flowing to your toes.

Resume normal activity. (For example, respond to the annoyance, but with an alert mind and a calm body. Was the worry worth a passing-gear response?)

With these steps of the QR sequence in mind, close your eyes and practice until you feel comfortable, then open your eyes and continue reading.

From now on, practice the six-second Quieting Response whenever you encounter an annoyance or anxiety. During subsequent sessions, we shall explore the step-by-step training exercises that will build to make the QR a fully automatic part of your daily life.

10. Session 2: Developing Tension Awareness——Clues and Cues for QR

In this session, you will learn how to scan your body for hidden clues that are signs of being tense and uptight. *Clues* are stress indicators that normally escape your attention but that you can become aware of through the QR training. By scanning your body, you may realize, for example, that you are clenching your jaw—a *clue* that you're experiencing stress. As you continue the training and develop your body awareness, you will notice such signals immediately and use them to call forth the conscious Quieting Response at the earliest possible moment— now these stress indicators have become *cues*. With further practice, these conscious cues will be gradually replaced by less obvious ones—the ultimate cue will be just a subtle change in your breathing pattern—that will call forth the automatic Quieting Reflex whenever stress is inappropriate, perhaps even during disturbing dreams.

The QR Diary Scan, which you have already begun using, is your guide for tuning in on your body. It makes you pause to check out your body and provides an orderly system for scanning the early signals of mounting tension. Daily use permits you to turn what have been hidden but nagging clues of tension into more obvious early warning signals that you are in danger of slipping unnecessarily into the emergency response, or passing gear. Each of these cues calls for a pause—a six-second QR—that will enable you to choose between the aroused emergency response or the balanced state of an alert mind in a calm body.

Ask yourself this question: "How did the stress of life trick me into slipping into perpetual passing gear, running down my body and fighting myself, rather than a real enemy?" Do you consciously, or even unconsciously, say to yourself, "If I try hard, I can do it"? Do you recall being told at home or school, "Come on, try hard; try harder"? If so, you'll find this reflected in your body. The resulting faulty bracing, or dysponesis, is akin to driving with one foot pushing down on the gas pedal and the other pushing down on the brake. Yet people often confuse their bodies with just such opposing commands.

Now rest your hands on the arms of your chair. Concentrate on an object, animal or person that bothers you. Scan the sensation in your body at this moment. Is it unpleasant? You are in the process of "mental faulty bracing." Now, still focusing on this unpleasant image, grasp the chair tightly with your hands. Hold. With your tense body and mind, resist this unpleasant image; brace against your thoughts. Now let go, and take an easy deep breath. Repeat this exercise, this time with your eyes closed, exhaling as you open your eyes.

Look for clues to what happened in your body. The unpleasant thoughts caused disquieting sensations within you as you inwardly braced. The muscles in your hands and wrists, arms, even your neck and shoulders are outwardly braced. In this exercise, you have intentionally adopted a faulty bracing position, but you do the same thing unconsciously many times a day.

Recall, for example, the way you have squirmed or braced when experiencing pain, trying to find some body position that minimizes the discomfort. Think of the people you see tightly clenching their steering wheels when they drive in traffic. People with backache and similar muscle and skeletal problems seem to experience a worsening of their conditions in the fall when the weather turns cold and in the spring when the weather turns warm. This pattern can be attributed to the rigid bracing posture people adopt as they shiver against the cold, and to the body's inability to let go again once the rigid posture is no longer needed.

Take a minute to tune in to what you do to your body when this happens. Place your hands and arms in a protective position by embracing your chest, as if you were protecting yourself from the cold. Try to shiver. Hold. Now look for faulty bracing cues. Notice the tension in your fingers, wrists and arms. Notice any discomfort in your shoulders and lower back. You are simply "trying too hard."

Trying too hard to get to sleep is another example of dysponesis. Chances are you become more restless and stay awake as you repeat to yourself, "I must get to sleep." Thus your body's remarkable capacity to recharge energy stores during sleep is overridden by your mental strategy of trying too hard.

QR teaches that you can have an alert mind and a calm body, minimizing the adverse effects of faulty bracing. In most situations, you'll find your alert mind can deal with life's pressures more effectively without the interference of an inappropriate passing-gear body. QR helps improve your mind's ability to observe your body and adopt a quiet inner amusement, even humor, when you realize you have let your body accidentally slip into passing gear. By quietly attending, not trying too hard, you foster a state of balance and harmony.

I would like you to play body detective now. I want you to find clues in your outward behavior that are indicators of your inward tension.

Make the following gestures to see if you recognize them as your own. Place one hand on the back of your neck. Try rubbing the tension away as you move your head from side to side. Do you often find yourself doing this?

Now tighten and then open your fists as if you are trying to get rid of tension. Do you do this?

Shrug your shoulders and move them around as if you are

trying to work out tired muscles. Sigh. Do you do this?

Now rub your cheeks and jaw with your hands to relieve pressure. Do you do this?

Do you bite your nails? Chew your lip? Clench your teeth? Jiggle your foot? Tap your fingers? These are just a few outward body clues to inward stress. If you frequently find yourself doing any of these things, you have a tension-stress problem that can be relieved by QR.

For a few moments, do a very general body-tension muscle scan. Take several easy, regular breaths. Think of your mind as a doctor-observer who can examine every part of your body. Begin your examination by passively scanning for clues of tension. As the following sentences describe, take a few seconds to focus on each part of your body. Move slowly, thoroughly considering each part in turn.

Begin by focusing on your toes, then the rest of your feet, and then your ankles.

Slowly move your attention up your legs to your calves, your kneecaps, to your thighs and buttocks.

Pay attention next to your abdomen and stomach.

Scan your chest, your ribs, your heart.

Focus now on your fingers, hands, knuckles, your wrists, forearms, elbows, upper arms, shoulders, your neck.

Next pay attention to your face, your forehead, eyes, mouth, tongue, jawbone, your entire head.

Have you noticed any tightness or discomfort?

Focus further now on your facial muscles, for the clues and cues to inward tension that can show outwardly in your face. Begin by making an exaggerated face: scrunch up your forehead and nose and twist your mouth. Hold for a second. You have made the cues of facial tension very obvious.

Let your facial muscles loose now. Think for a second of the last time someone said to you, "What's the matter?" and you responded, "Nothing, why?" What cues to inward tension or distress were you transmitting to others by outward facial tension?

Wrinkle your eyebrows. Were you doing that? Rest.

Flare your nostrils. Were you doing that? Rest.

Gently grit your teeth. Rest. Frown slightly. Rest. Were you doing either of those?

People often brace their facial muscles unconsciously. The face is a unique gearshift mechanism that provides clues about how you are feeling inside. Are you annoyed, worried or afraid? QR will let you "gear down" your facial muscles.

Make another exaggerated face.

Now, consciously try to gear down your face, beginning with your forehead. Let go of tension there, then down through your eyes, through your nose, and to the sides of your face by your ears. Relax the sides of your cheeks and jaw, loosen the tension in your mouth, and let your entire jaw go loose and drop. That is one way to gear down your facial muscles.

Let's move now to your diaphragm, which is used in breathing, to scan for clues and cues to inward tension that are evident in your breathing pattern. Interruption of a slow, regular breathing pattern is a clue that something is disturbing your breathing balance. When you throw your body into inappropriate passing gear, you throw your breathing into inappropriate breathing gear. Now, as an example, gasp and clutch your chest. Notice your breathing pattern. Is it irregular?

Now try another simple exercise. You will have to look away from the page to do it, so read the instructions first. Thinking the word *tick*, focus your eyes on the upper right corner of the ceiling. Then thinking *tock*, focus on the left corner of the ceiling. Repeat a couple of times. Okay, do it now, moving just your eyes, not your head.

Notice that your breathing stopped for a few seconds. You suddenly asked your mind to become aware of something—stage one of the emergency response—and you experienced a catch or holding of your breath, which is stage three of the emergency response. When we direct people's attention to anything, they will almost always catch their breath; a small percentage of people will start breathing faster.

Next, place one hand on your chest and the other on your abdomen and concentrate on slow, deliberate breaths. Breathe in: *one, two, three*. Breathe out: *one, two, three*. In. Out. What do you notice? Your breathing is slow, deliberate and regular. Wiggle your fingers.

Think for a few seconds about how often you throw your breathing pattern into passing gear when something startles you out of deep concentration or when free-floating anxiety or anger causes you to clench your teeth and jaw.

During the beginning stages of the QR training, you need to enhance your awareness of body cues of tension, time pressure, worry or anger, to become more sensitive to early cues that can eventually lead to stress symptoms or pain. Recognizing these signs of inward tension will enable you to choose the best body gear for the stress at hand.

Continue with your daily QR Diary Scan and Quieting Responses—but put the book aside now for five days before proceeding to Session 3, separating subsequent sessions by approximately five-day intervals.

Do a QR now.

11. Session 3:   Breathing, the Foundation of QR

Assume as comfortable a sitting position as possible. Think of your body as having the strength and stability of a pyramid, the foundation of which is breathing. At this foundation level, you will become aware of the importance of quiet, regular breathing. Then, with practice, subtle changes in breathing, even during sleep, will become the automatic cue for the Quieting Reflex.

Breathing is the basic rhythm of life. The newborn's first breath signals life's beginning; the last breath marks its end. Breath nourishes not only the body but the brain, which is the seat of the nervous system. Breathing has been the cornerstone of self-regulation techniques like yoga throughout history, because when we alter our breathing, we alter our consciousness and our life momentarily. Alterations in our normal breathing rhythm changes the amount of oxygen available to the brain.

The mixture of oxygen and other gases is in delicate balance, and even subtle changes in it change our consciousness.

When we experience the emergency response, our breathing is one of the very first functions to change, and it often does so entirely without our awareness. Thus a key part of learning QR is noticing your breathing.

Focus now on the way your chest and shoulders move as you breathe. Notice the length of your inhalation and of your exhalation.

When you change the way you breathe, you change the way you feel. Remember a time when you've been in passing gear, perhaps running a distance or exercising hard so that you were panting. Now place one hand on your chest and the other on your abdomen and pant for five short breaths. Notice your breathing pattern and movement. Drop your hands.

Your breathing has changed, and you are experiencing other feelings of excitement along with that change in breathing; for example, your face may feel hot. What most people don't realize is that we frequently change our breathing unconsciously, thereby altering our thoughts and mood.

Again place one hand on your chest and the other on your abdomen, and for just a few seconds, deliberately put your breathing mechanism into passing gear—breathe rapidly. Let the areas behind your hands move up and down and in and out as fast as you can breathe. Rest.

Now tighten your shoulders slightly and gently clench your teeth as you breathe fast. Notice the bracing effort in your shoulders, your chest, and your neck and facial area. Now rest, briefly wiggle your fingers and think about your sensations.

As you were breathing that way, could you remember times when you felt scared, panicked, upset or angry? Think for a moment of a time within the last day or two when you experienced anger or fear or were upset.

Recall your physical reaction.

Did you overreact to the situation?

Did your body go into passing gear inappropriately?

Now try to feel an inner amusement toward that experience. Smile with your eyes and mouth. Now break into a great big real smile. Drop your jaw and release the tension from your face, noticing the release. Keep smiling with your eyes, thinking with inner amusement of how inappropriate your uptight breathing was.

Now I want you to experience another breathing sensation, that of gearing down your breathing mechanism, rather than gearing up. Again with one hand on your chest and the other on your abdomen, inhale slowly. Feel your ribs expand, and at the same time, raise your torso, lifting your rib cage up "off" your hip bones. Hold your breath.

You should be aware of an expanded sensation of space in your abdomen and should feel your spine gently stretching. Now, open your mouth slightly and deliberately exhale, allowing a small portion of the air in your chest cavity to remain.

Inhale again, filling the abdomen and the entire chest cavity. Allow full action of the breathing mechanism, so that you experience an expansion of your entire chest cavity and a feeling of expansion up the back of your neck and through your shoulders into your head, arms and hands and down into your lower torso to your legs and feet. Now exhale with a deliberate slow movement, allowing your breath to flow out but still maintaining a little air in your upper chest.

Practice for a few minutes. Continue to inhale slowly and deeply, then exhale. See if you can take a deep breath that fills your abdomen so that your lower hand actually moves, and let the air out slowly and completely. Monitor your breathing by focusing on your hand's movement.

Try it again: take a slow, deep, easy breath, then let the air back out slowly and easily. Slightly part your lips and let go of the tightness in your jaw and tongue. Take one more easy breath.

How do you feel now?

As you practice quiet, easy breathing, you may begin to notice some tightness in your back or elsewhere in your body. This is not a cause for alarm. It is merely your breath expanding to release areas that were formerly bound by muscle tension. Rest for a moment and consider the physical movement in your breathing.

When you exhale, your shoulders can go loose, but it is important not to allow an exaggerated downward motion in the collarbone area. Such a collapse or slouch causes the rib cage to become cramped, resulting in a crowding and squashing of your internal organs. Each organ has its own space, its "orbit." When you exhale properly, the upper chest cavity retains some air. Pushing all the air out is "trying too hard" and can cause congestion and more tension. With each gentle inhalation, remember to lift your rib cage off your hip bones, creating more space for your inner organs.

You will be practicing this slow, easy breathing over and over in the QR exercises. You can already sense that as you change your breathing, you change how you feel. When you regulate your breathing, you feel quiet, peaceful and calm. By altering your breathing rhythm, you can adjust your level of body activation to whatever stress confronts you.

The next steps expand the breathing exercise. This is an unusual and remarkably effective way for both children and adults to experience almost all of the QR sensations.

Smile inwardly. Say to yourself, "My body is calm." Wiggle your toes a couple of times.

Now place one hand on your chest and the other on your abdomen.

Focus your mind on your toes.

Now on the bottoms of your feet.

Imagine that you have "breathing pores" in the bottoms of your feet. Feel the imaginary breathing pores.

Now, through the breathing pores, pull good clean air in through the bottoms of your feet.

Let the air move through your toes, inside your feet, through your ankles, up through your calves, up your legs past your kneecaps and through your thighs to fill your abdomen. Now push a feeling of heaviness and warmth from your stomach down through your thighs, your knees, your calves, your ankles, and out through your breathing pores. You may wish to repeat this exercise, tracing the breathing pathway with your fingertips, beginning at your toes. Rest for a moment.

Wiggle your toes. Smile inwardly. Say to yourself, "My body is calm." Again breathe in through the breathing pores in the bottoms of your feet, letting clean fresh air travel to your toes, ankles, calves, knees, thighs and abdomen. Now push heaviness and warmth back through your thighs, knees, calves, ankles, toes and out through the breathing pores in your feet.

Smile inwardly with your eyes and mouth. Give your body the suggestion, "My body is calm." This time, you will count as you breathe. Wiggle your toes. Breathe in: *one, two, three.* Breathe out: *one, two, three.*

As described in Session 1, dropping your jaw as you exhale to relieve tension is a crucial part of QR. Place your hands now on the sides of your face, cupping your cheeks and jaw.

Focus on the warmth of your hands.

Slightly open and close your mouth.

Now, as you open your mouth, feel your jaw drop, becoming looser and less tense. Let the flowing limpness loosen any tight feelings.

Feel the warmth of your fingers and hands help move your jaw into a loose position.

Now place your hands at your sides. Slowly drop your jaw again and feel flowing warmth and looseness. Wiggle your fingers and toes. Use this exercise often to encourage awareness of unconscious jaw tension.

Now you are ready to do the complete six-second QR, but before you do, review the process. Remember that first you will smile inwardly and with your eyes and mouth, saying to yourself, "Alert mind, calm body." Next, you will breathe in through the breathing pores in your feet, then drop your jaw, tongue and shoulders and breathe out.

As a trial run, use your hand to trace the movement of your inhalation and exhalation. Ready? With your hand close to your body, let your hand flow up your body as you inhale, then down your body as you exhale. Move your hand up as you inhale; drop your jaw; move your hand down as you exhale.

This movement will help you pace your breathing and experientially trace the inward path of flowing air on the inhalation and the outward flow of heaviness and warmth on the exhalation. Close your eyes now and repeat this exercise, taking your time, until you are comfortable with it. Then open your eyes and rest for a moment.

Now do your QR with one hand placed lightly on your chest and the other on your abdomen. Wiggle your toes. Smile inwardly and with your eyes and mouth, saying to yourself, "Alert mind, calm body." Focus on the breathing pores in your feet. Ready? Breathe in: *one, two, three;* drop your jaw; breathe out: *one, two, three.*

Again: smile inwardly; breathe in; and drop your jaw as you breathe out. Repeat with your eyes closed. Then open your eyes and wiggle your toes and fingers.

Learning to regulate your breathing is important for releasing tension, but combining deliberate inhaling and exhaling with the very important step of dropping your jaw helps make QR unique and especially effective.

Practice your QR before you go to sleep or before you get out of bed in the morning. At these times, practice with your eyes closed. Place your hands on your chest and abdomen; wiggle your toes and fingers. Smile inwardly and with your eyes and mouth, saying to yourself, "Alert mind, calm body." Breathe in through your breathing pores. Experience the flowing warmth and heaviness in each part of your body that you focused on today. Let your tongue and jaw gently go loose as you exhale. During the day, while sitting or standing, pause to practice your QR with your eyes open. Begin to practice it any time, anywhere, so that it will become a natural response to annoyance, worry or fear.

12. Session 4: Skeletal Muscles, Heaviness and QR

Let's begin this session by doing a six-second QR. Do your QR with your eyes closed, but first review the instructions: Place your body in a comfortable position. Wiggle your toes and focus on your imaginary breathing pores. Recall that you will pull in warm, flowing air through your breathing pores to your ankles, calves and knees, up to your thighs and to your abdomen, then reverse the pathway. Recall that a crucial step is the combined exhalation and jaw drop, including loosening your tongue and shoulders.

Are you ready? First, do a brief tongue thrust as a cue. Now smile inwardly with your mouth and eyes, and think of having an alert mind and a calm body. Breathe in: *one, two, three;* drop your jaw; breathe out: *one, two, three*. Now close your eyes and do the QR again.

As you develop your automatic Quieting Reflex, the next

building block of the pyramid involves increasing body awareness and balancing the voluntary, or skeletal muscles—those muscles used to move the skeleton, the eyes and the vocal cords. As described in Chapter 2, movement of the skeletal muscles is normally under voluntary control, but the levels of basic tension in them are maintained by the unconscious gamma efferent system. Because of unconscious mental factors or the stress and strain of life, people learn to overset the gamma efferent system, making the skeletal muscles too taut, a condition that can cause or aggravate fatigue, headache and backache. As you acquire skills in permitting your skeletal muscles to stay in harmonious balance through daily practice of the six-second QR, you will experience brief sensations of flowing heaviness in your body, usually beginning in your face, the muscles of which we have already noted a skeletal-muscle gearshift mechanism between voluntary and involuntary control.

The first exercise in this session focuses on extending muscle quieting from the face to other muscle groups in the body. Begin with a muscle-tension body scan. Take several easy, regular breaths. Think of your mind as a kind of doctor-observer who can examine every part of your body. Begin by passively scanning for any clues of tension. Whenever you do note clues of tightness or discomfort, smile to yourself and continue. First focus on your toes, then your entire feet. Move up to your ankles, then to your calves, your kneecaps, your thighs, your abdomen and stomach. Focus on your chest, your ribs, the area around your heart. Focus on your fingers, your knuckles, your whole hands, your wrists, your forearms, your elbows, your upper arms, your shoulders, your neck. Focus on your face, your forehead, your eyes, your mouth, your tongue, your jaw and your entire head.

You can improve the skill with which you scan muscle tension by using an exercise that contrasts tension and release. Settle into a comfortable sitting position, then focus on each part of your body and follow the experiential directions described in the succeeding sentences.

Begin your muscle-tension scan by noticing tense feelings in your fingers, hands and wrists. Explore this tension area.

Wiggle your fingers. Slowly scrunch up the fingers of one hand into a tight fist.

Tighten your fingers into your palm as hard as you can.

Notice what it feels like when the muscles in your hand, wrist and arm are trembling and tense.

Now deliberately release your fingers, floating them apart. Let the hand float into a heavy, loose position. Notice the feeling in your hand, wrist and arm now.

Notice how they feel different from your other hand, wrist and arm.

You are experiencing what it feels like when you let your skeletal muscles become very loose and heavy. The hand-arm area is one in which baseline tension can easily be overset.

Try the same exercise again, but this time use both hands. Wiggle your fingers. Raise both arms slightly and straighten them. Deliberately scrunch the fingers of both hands into tight fists.

Keep tightening your fingers. Squeeze hard to tighten your wrists and arm muscles. Hold for several seconds.

Now float your fists open. Let the muscles and tension go as you float your arms to your sides. Notice the wonderful feeling of heaviness and limpness in your arms as they sink.

Notice how different your arms, wrists and hands feel when they're heavy and loose.

What you've just experienced is a basic contrast between tensing and relaxing, which will help you discriminate between tight and loose sensations and encourage pleasant, heavy, flowing feelings in these tense areas.

Next, with your dominant hand—right if you're right-handed—rub the upper part of the opposite arm as you make a fist and slightly flex the upper-arm muscle.

Move your hand over the tightened area up to your shoulder. Notice the tightening in your arm and shoulder.

Now, with both hands, grasp your shoulders. Raise your shoulders up toward your ears and curl your chin down, as if you're trying to hide by pulling your head into your chest. Make your shoulders tight and very tense. Hold this position for a second.

Now let loose. Drop your shoulders. Return your hands to a comfortable position. Focus on the feelings of flowing looseness as they extend through your neck and shoulders. Rest for a moment.

This time, leave your hands by your sides. Raise your shoulders toward your ears in a tense posture. Hold the tension.

Now exhale and deliberately push the tension from your shoulders, neck and arms, down through your chest, abdomen and legs, and out the breathing pores in your feet. Focus on the release of tension. Rest again for a few seconds.

Again raise your shoulders. Hold.

Now exhale and push out the tension through your entire body. Wiggle your fingers.

With the fingers of one hand, gently rub the back of your neck. The entire neck and shoulder area is vulnerable to unconscious bracing against anxiety and annoyance. During the day, notice if you catch yourself rubbing these areas. When you do, do a QR to release your tension.

Do a QR now. Wiggle your toes. Ready? Smile inwardly and with your mouth and eyes; think, "Alert mind, calm body." Breathe in: *one, two, three*. Drop your jaw. Breathe out: *one, two, three*. Think, "My body feels calm."

Next, focus on your facial muscles, which are frequently involved in producing wrinkles and a grim countenance when you are unconsciously tense. Gently rub your nose with your fingers.

Scrunch up your nose and let your fingers slide up the hard bony area between your eyes. Focus on this tense, bracing attitude.

Now move your fingers carefully around your eyebrows and eye muscles, particularly around the sides of each eye. Notice the tension.

Rest for a moment. Very gently rub the entire area between your eyes and ears in a circular motion. Concentrate on gearing down and releasing tension in this area.

Move your fingers across your cheekbones to your nose and back to your ears. Now gently slide your fingers from the top of your ears to the bone just in front of each ear. Keep your fingers on this spot. It is called the temporomandibular joint, or simply the TMJ. This joint between the temples and jaw is located on each side of your face just in front of your earlobes. With fingers in place, slowly open your mouth wide.

Now, slowly close your mouth. Carefully open your mouth. Carefully close your mouth. Feel the movement in the TMJ area.

When you grimace, scowl, or clench or grind your teeth because of anger or annoyance, tension is placed on the TMJ. This is a major tension site in about 20 percent of the population. Releasing tension from this area by dropping your jaw and loosening your tongue is vital to achieving optimal benefit from the six-second QR. Take a few seconds now to gently move your jaw with one hand to relieve pressure from the TMJ area.

To complete this exploration of facial tension, do a QR. This time, deliberately focus on the importance of the jaw drop in releasing tension from the TMJ area. Permit your eyes to close now, do a QR, and then open your eyes.

Move your awareness next to your chest and back, also areas in which you may increase tension through inappropriate gearing up. Inhale a deep breath. Hold the breath, feeling the uncomfortable pressure against your chest and back. Now exhale slowly and deliberately to release the tension. Notice the sensation. Breath holding or inappropriate irregular breathing increases muscle discomfort. Now take in a comfortable, even, deep breath and exhale an easy, deep breath. Inhale. Exhale. Feel your chest and neck muscles becoming limp. Feel yourself becoming heavier and calmer. Move your fingers and toes.

Continue to feel each part of your body become even looser and heavier as you breathe. One by one, feel each body part melting, sinking and becoming even heavier and easier. First, release the tension in your face. Smile inwardly with your eyes and mouth.

Loosen your tongue.

Drop your jaw.

Loosen your shoulders.

Feel the flow—let your stomach loose.

Let the looseness flow through your thighs, calves, feet and toes.

Feel your entire body, including your arms and fingers, becoming more and more heavy and quiet.

Remain still for a moment, feeling completely heavy and completely calm.

Smile inwardly with your mouth and eyes, and couple the sensation of flowing, heavy air from quiet breathing with reduced muscle tension in different areas of your body. Recognize that you can use breathing to "exhale" muscle tension, permitting it to flow out of your body.

Starting now, whenever you encounter annoyances, use your alert, overseeing mind to observe your muscle tension, breathing pattern, mood and feelings to detect any disguised clues of tension. Imagine that you are viewing the lower levels of a pyramid from its peak.

You can do this at any time during the day—each time the phone rings, for example, or each time you hang up the phone, or, when driving, each time you pause for a traffic light. Make it a game—whenever you encounter an annoyance, observe your breathing and your jaw and fist tension. Is your breathing shallow or short, or are you holding your breath, or are you breathing with just your chest? Quietly observe how your breathing pattern reflects your state of muscle tension as well as your mood and feelings.

If you find signs of tension, do a QR. Smile to yourself; suggest inwardly, "Alert mind, calm body"; breathe in, and then let your tongue, jaw and shoulders drop as you breathe out.

13. Session 5: Smooth Muscles, Warming and QR

Before proceeding with this session, think for a few moments of situations or experiences that have made you feel warm and secure. An example is sunning on the beach on a pleasant day. List a few such situations on a piece of paper.

Now do a brief body scan to identify any areas of muscle tension.

Next, smile inwardly, telling yourself, "Alert mind, calm body." Smile with your eyes and mouth. Part your lips to loosen your "smile muscles." Feel your face as calm and loose. Gently move your toes. Now breathe in slowly and deeply through the imaginary pores in the bottoms of your feet. Pull the air into your ankles, then up into your legs through your calves, your kneecaps and thighs, through your abdomen, to your upper rib cage, and up around your neck and shoulders. Now deliberately push warm air back down through your shoulders, letting them go loose with a heavy, calm sensation, at the same time letting your jaw drop and your tongue go loose. Push the heaviness, warmth and limpness back down through your ribs, abdomen, thighs, knees, calves and ankles, and then push the air and tension out.

Continue this quieting process for about thirty seconds, letting your jaw drop each time you exhale. Experience the heaviness, warmth and limpness.

Observe your mood and feelings, noticing that as your breathing becomes quieter, your body muscles become less tense.

Repeat this exercise with your eyes closed. When you feel comfortable with it, open your eyes and continue reading.

Continue to experience the feeling of heaviness, warmth and limpness as you read about the next level of the QR pyramid. In the last session, you related a sensation of flowing *heaviness* to an awareness of *skeletal-muscle* tension flowing out of your body with your breathing. In this session, you will relate the sensation of flowing *warmth* to the other major kind of body muscle, *smooth muscle*. Smooth muscles encircle your blood vessels, your digestive system and the air passages in your lungs. They are normally not under voluntary control, and if they go into spasm, they can produce cold hands and feet, migraine headache, high blood pressure, heart pain, difficult breathing or digestive upset. The sensation of flowing warmth, coupled with QR breathing, helps prevent the smooth muscles from going into spasm.

Think back to the images that make you feel warm and secure that you wrote down at the beginning of this session. Concentrate now on the image you remember best.

Let your mind focus on the objects within this warm, safe image.

For the next minute, breathe quietly, letting your image fill your thoughts and mind.

Now let your warm safe image embrace your body with feelings of flowing warmth. Let the image mingle with your deep, regular breathing.

Your body is calm and quiet.

Gently move your toes and fingers.

Close your eyes and repeat the exercise; then open your eyes and continue.

Maintaining this inner sense of calm and security, direct your attention to your hands. Rub your thumbs along your fingertips.

Now tighten your fingers and clench your fists. Study your hand posture.

Study the tight knuckles.

Notice the tight feeling in your wrists, and then in your forearms.

Release one fist and rub the fingers over the tight fist and knuckles of the other hand.

Rub the wrist area. Study the tense posture.

Keep your fist tight and raise it to your lips. Try to blow some warm body air into your clenched fist.

If you have really clenched your hand tightly, you will be unable to get any air through it. The inability to push your warm body air into your fist symbolizes how one natural body process—breathing—is altered by muscle tensing. Unclench your fist, wiggle your fingers and rest a moment.

Now make another tight fist and again place it in front of your lips. Imagine that your clenched fist is a balloon that wants to expand but cannot do so.

Slowly and deliberately blow some warm body air into your fist until it feels as warm as it can get, then permit your fingers to expand like the sides of a balloon. Use your exhaled body warmth to open and release your tense fingers.

Feel the warmth and release of tension as your fingers float freely away from your lips and jaw.

Let your heavy, warm hand return to your side. Notice your feelings.

This exercise helps you transfer the quiet warmth of your breath to your smooth muscles, to give them an idea of how to be less tense. Loose smooth muscles produce a sensation of flowing warmth. Repeat this exercise again with your eyes closed.

Now let's extend flowing heaviness and warmth into other parts of your body.

First, take a couple of quiet, easy breaths.

Let your mind focus on your feet, then on your toes, on the soles of your feet and on your special breathing pores.

Pull air up through your breathing pores, then through your ankles, calves, knees and thighs, to fill your abdomen.

Now gently and deliberately breathe out, feeling the flowing heaviness and warmth moving inside your body back to your feet.

Below is a list of phrases for you to repeat inwardly. As you say each phrase to yourself, direct your attention to the specific body part mentioned. Concentrate on sending warmth to each body part as you inwardly name it. Pause after each phrase and give yourself time to experience the sensations in the body part mentioned. Read slowly, closing your eyes to repeat each phrase before going on to the next. Say to yourself:

"My ankles and calves feel heavy and warm."
"My knees and thighs feel heavy and warm."
"My abdomen feels heavy and warm."
"I am breathing slowly and deeply."
"My hands feel heavy and warm."
"My wrists and forearms feel heavy and warm."
"My elbows and upper arms feel heavy and warm."
"My shoulders feel heavy and warm."
"My neck feels heavy and warm."
"My eyes, my forehead, my cheeks, my mouth and my jaw feel heavy and warm."
"My whole body feels heavy and warm."
"My breathing is slow, deep and safe."
"I feel safe and calm."

Now read the following sentences slowly, again repeating each to yourself before going on to the next:

"My head feels warm from my body warmth."
"The warmth in the top of my head is beginning to slowly flow down into my forehead, through my eyes, to my mouth and jaw, and gently through my neck."
"The warmth moves down into my right shoulder, and now

the warmth flows down my upper arm, calming the tension in my elbow."

"The warmth is flowing down my forearm to my wrist, moving through the knuckles, flowing warmth into my hand and now into my fingers."

"My right hand feels heavy and warm."

"My head is cooling and becoming more alert as the heat flows down to my warming hand, which is becoming calm and heavy."

"The warmth slowly flows up my arm into my right shoulder."

"The warmth is moving up my arm into my right shoulder, gently bringing flowing warmth through my neck and across into my left shoulder."

"The warmth is flowing into my left shoulder, down my left upper arm."

"Now warmth encircles my left elbow, flowing down my forearm to my wrist, moving through my knuckles, flowing warmth into my hand and into my fingers."

"My left hand feels heavy and warm."

"Now the flowing warmth moves back up my left arm into my left shoulder and to my heart."

"The calm, secure warmth gently encircles my heart."

"My heart feels warm and safe."

"My heartbeat is slow and regular and safe."

"Now I sense the flowing warmth moving down from my heart to my abdomen."

"I am breathing more deeply and calmly, and I feel the warmth beginning to flow from my stomach through my hips."

"Now the warmth is flowing slowly through my thighs, my knees, my calves, my ankles and my feet."

"My feet are heavy and warm."

"My breathing is calmer and deeper."

"The warmth flows into my feet and then begins to flow back up my legs, through my abdomen, my chest and back up into my heart with each breath."

"My heart feels warm and easy."

"My heart sends warmth through my whole body."

"My whole body is heavy, warm, quiet and safe."

"My body feels quiet, limp, heavy, calm and safe."

"My mind is cool and alert."

"My body is heavy and warm and my mind is cool."

Slowly move your toes.

Slowly move your fingers.

Pause a few seconds to look for body cues with a muscle-tension body scan, contrasting your warm feelings now with the tensions you felt before you began. Conclude this session by doing a QR.

14. Session 6: Combining QR Elements

In this session, you will review and combine the elements of the QR into an integrated exercise.

Permit your body to find as comfortable a sitting position as possible.

Step One is a *cue*, an awareness of tension, of being uptight. This cue can be as obvious as the sensation caused by thrusting your tongue against the top of your mouth, or by a sore neck or back muscle, or it can be much more subtle, like a feeling of not wanting to answer the phone or of being under too much time pressure. Your awareness of such subtle cues is becoming more sensitive through your use of the QR Diary Scan, which helps you detect when you are accidentally slipping into passing gear.

Everything that follows the cue is a response to that cue, and with practice, the response will become automatic. The suceeding steps are:

Step Two: Smile inwardly. Smile with your eyes and mouth. Give yourself the suggestion, "Alert mind, calm body."

Step Three: Inhale an easy, deep breath through the imaginary breathing pores in your feet. Let the image of warm air flow up through your feet, ankles, calves, knees, thighs and up into your torso, giving your inner organs space to function.

Step Four: As you exhale, let your jaw, tongue and shoulders go loose, feeling a wave of heaviness and warmth wash all the tension out of your face, neck, shoulders, arms, chest, abdomen, legs, ankles, feet and toes.

Resume normal activity.

As you continue this session, try to deepen your awareness of the six-second QR.

Imagine now that you are climbing aboard your own very safe space ship.

Feel your body sitting down in the control chair.

Imagine that because you are a little uptight, you do a QR. Do it now.

Now that you are comfortable, imagine the objects in your space ship.

You are about to lift off, shifting gears up with your QR for an appropriate reaction to stress.

You are taking off.

You are beginning to feel the increasing gravity.

You feel the pressure against you.

Your body is tense.

Grip the arms of your chair to brace against the force of gravity.

Inhale a deep breath. Hold it.

Your whole body is getting more and more tense.

Tighten your toes, feet and legs.

Tighten your fingers, arms and shoulders.

Tighten your neck and face.

Hold on! You are tight and tense; the gravity is increasing; the tension is growing harder and tighter.

Now as you suddenly burst through the gravity field, exhale deeply.

You're weightless. Your whole body loosens.

Let your jaw, tongue and shoulders go loose.

Let your eyes smile.

Let your neck and shoulders go loose.

Your arms and fingers go limp. Your abdomen, thighs and legs go loose.

Your ankles, feet and toes are heavy and loose and warm.

Feel your muscles letting go as you float.

Your body is weightless and safe.

You feel serene.

Say to yourself, "Alert mind, effortless body." Notice how you feel when your muscles let go—when you feel calm and serene.

Your body has now floated safely back to where you began. You feel heavy, safe and calm.

Your body is sinking deeper and deeper into your chair.

You feel heavy and calm.

Stay completely motionless.

Without actually doing it, think about lifting up one leg.

Think about the muscles that you would have to use if you were to raise your leg. Think about the muscles that you would have to use if you were to raise your arm. Notice the tensions that have crept into these muscles just because of your thoughts. Thoughts can invade your muscles to make you feel tense or to make you feel calm.

As you read the following sentences, feel heaviness and warmth flowing to each body part; at the same time sink comfortably into your chair. Feel a quiet joy and a sense of self-mastery as you say to yourself:

"My body is calm."

"My forehead, my eyes and my mouth feel loose."

"My jaw and tongue feel loose as I slowly open my mouth."

"My neck and shoulders feel heavy and loose."

"The heaviness and warmth moves down my arms, to my wrists and then to my fingers."

"Heaviness and warmth surround my chest; my heart is warm."

"My abdomen feels heavy."

"Heaviness and warmth move through my thighs and down my legs."

"Heaviness and warmth move through my knees and calves to surround my ankles."

"Now my feet are heavy and warm."

"My body is calm."

"My breathing is slow and regular."

"I breathe in and think, Q."

"I breathe out and think, R."

"I breathe in: Q."

I breathe out: R."

Be still for a few seconds.

Practice this exercise until you are comfortable with it. Gently wiggle your toes. Move your fingers.

In the final exercises in this session, you will experience a deepening awareness of heaviness and warmth.

Picture a blank screen, like a movie screen.

Bring your palms together in front of your chest.

Now rub your hands together, creating warmth.

Move your palms about an inch apart and sense that the warmth continues to flow across the open space between them.

Now move your palms to your mouth and transfer the heat from your breath to your hands. Gently blow between your palms to feel flowing warmth. When your palms seem about as warm as they can become, move your palms to the sides of your face, without quite touching your cheeks. Feel the transfer of flowing warmth passing through your head, illuminating the imaginary screen.

This flow of warmth should make it easier for you to form an image of a blank screen. When you can picture the screen, let your hands settle in your lap.

Now let the screen dissolve into a calm flowing mist. Heaviness and warmth support your body as your mind sees clearly, penetrating the fog, like a headlight giving you a serene overview and control that is not at the mercy of your body. With your eyes closed, repeat this step until you're comfortable, then open your eyes and continue.

The exercise that follows is the QR Bedtime Daily Review. In it, I will ask you, without involving your body, to use your mind screen to play back the events of your day, like a movie running slowly in reverse, beginning with the most recent events and moving backward. Note time pressures, tensions and frustrations, but try not to judge yourself or others as bad or good. Instead, whenever your body signals a cue of increased tension, dissolve it with a six-second QR and proceed. Put the book down now and do a Daily Review for about five minutes. Then resume reading.

Many people who have already learned the QR technique have reported that such a daily review has had a dramatic impact on their sense of time pressure. The review helps them sort out behaviors and pressures that add to their sense of time urgency without being productive. Common reports are, "The daily review helped dissolve and resolve lingering experiences that normally would have kept me awake at night," and, "I wake up in the morning with a nagging problem solved—the solution seemed to come to me while I had a marvelous sleep."

Because of these enthusiastic reports, I have formalized this procedure in the QR Bedtime Daily Review, an eight-step exercise that you should memorize and use at bedtime whenever possible. It incorporates and integrates many aspects of QR training with the daily review.

Some nights you may be too tired to complete or even to begin it. There is no reason to be concerned if you fall asleep while carrying out its steps. In fact, falling asleep indicates that the six-second QR that you have been practicing with each annoyance during the day is dissolving your stress so effectively that the daily review is not necessary.

The QR Bedtime Daily Review follows:

Step 1: Rate today's activities on your QR Diary Scan.
Step 2: Lie down in bed with your eyes closed.

Step 3: Hold your hands in front of you as if you were praying. Take a deep breath, and, holding it, press your hands together until you can feel your arm muscles begin to tremble. Maintain this trembling as long as you can, and then breathe out, letting your hands fall to your sides completely limp.

Step 4: Take another deep breath and hold it, slowly drawing your hands toward your face. When your hands touch your face, rest them there and breathe out, letting yourself go completely limp.

Step 5: Move your hands to lightly cup your mouth while you carry out quiet, easy breathing for about half a minute. Feel the warmth of your exhaled breath warming your hands and then flowing down your arms, spilling through your shoulders to flow through your whole body.

Step 6: As you sense flowing heaviness and warmth in your legs, permit your warm hands to slowly leave your mouth and rest on your abdomen or legs. Continue your quiet, easy breathing.

Step 7: With your eyes still closed, gently focus on an imaginary point just in front of the tip of your nose and imagine that your nose is leading you through a cloud of floating mist that fills your mind like a blank movie screen.

Step 8: Now, with your mind like a blank screen, conduct your daily review. See the activities of your day running backward on the screen, observing them without judgment unless an annoyance creeps in. If one does, dissolve it with a six-second QR and continue.

15. Session 7: Balancing Distress With QR

The QR skill seeks to balance a grounded, calm body with an alert, attentive mind functioning at its best. It fully recognizes that healthy stress and positive tension are often desirable for optimal performance. With QR, your mind possesses a means to choose the best body gear to accomplish the task at hand.

QR, however, *can* fail you. If you're experiencing a sharp pain—as the result of a sudden blow, or a toothache, for example—it can be difficult to develop the sense of amusement and other attitudes that make the six-second QR work. In addition, some people who have used QR successfully to overcome such problems as headache, excessive perspiration or nervous stomach slip back into a pattern of trying too hard to make QR work—the very tendency QR taught them to avoid—and they may reexperience their problems.

What can you do if physical illness, distress, pain or tension beyond your control seeps down into your body structure, making it difficult for you to experience the six-second QR? What if you are aware of an annoying cue, but the flowing heaviness and warmth won't come?

The answer is to use the mental image of an elevator to move "down" to the level of the QR pyramid that still provides stability for you; then to ascend slowly, level by level, to fine-tuned balance. Whenever you feel you've lost control of your body, or experience a general feeling of instability, uneasiness or pain, remember QR and your ability to reach into yourself to draw upon the resources of your body. Keep in mind the idea that your body is as stable and enduring as a pyramid and your mind is the fine pinnacle above the broad foundation. From its height, you have the power, through images, to move slowly and positively to all levels of body function. You can reach into the organ spaces of your body to free them from cramping and congestion. You can send flowing warmth to muscle spasms, to your heart, to any place that hurts. You can create feelings of heaviness and warmth and release tension with breathing.

You can use the image of a mental elevator to move from the pinnacle to the base of your pyramid, the breathing level. Focus now on your body, a stable pyramid, the pinnacle of which is your alert mind.

Try using your mental elevator now to move down through your body—first to your neck, your shoulders and your arms.

Continue down to your midsection—your chest and abdomen—then farther down to your thighs and legs. Now, at your feet, begin to move your elevator upward, bringing back clean pure air through the imaginary breathing pores in your feet, coupling your mind to your breathing.

Close your eyes and repeat this exercise, progressing slowly. When you feel comfortable with it, open your eyes and continue.

As your breathing becomes smooth and soothing, your second pyramid level is heaviness—flowing heaviness.

Next, your mental elevator continues slowly upward as you experience the third level, flowing warmth.

Now, as the elevator climbs, you feel the combined breathing, heaviness and warmth, the top level of a balanced QR.

(The British word for elevator is "lift," and you might think of this balancing technique as a "lift" procedure, helping you ascend the QR pyramid on those occasions when you have slipped into an uncomfortable passing-gear state.)

Now practice moving to different levels within your body to balance QR with distress.

Remember a time when you were feeling pain.

Do a painful tongue thrust and clench your fists and toes. Notice the tension as it begins to dominate you, to occupy all the spaces of your body organs as you brace against it, as you hold your breath or breathe too hard.

Imagine that, given these tension cues, you try a QR, but it doesn't seem to work.

When this happens, call forth your mental elevator image, directing your entire mind to the level that makes you feel better.

The foundation level is quiet, regular breathing while you passively attend to the smooth, regular rhythm of your diaphragm. Place one hand on your chest. Place the other on your abdomen. Monitor your breathing pattern. Ignore everything else.

For a few minutes, merge your mind into the breathing level of your body pyramid. Take slow, deep, regular breaths. Ignore everything else.

Close your eyes and repeat this exercise until you experience slow, deep, regular breaths, then open your eyes and continue.

As you begin to feel a little better, think about the breathing pores in your feet. Smile inwardly. Give yourself the suggestion, "My body is calm."

Let your mind focus on your toes.

Now on the bottoms of your feet.

Imagine that you have breathing pores in the bottoms of your feet. Pull in good clean air through the breathing pores.

Totally occupy your mind with the movement of air through your toes, inside your feet, flowing through your ankles, up through your calves, up through your legs to surround your kneecaps, on up through your thighs, filling up first your abdomen and then the area of discomfort. Now exhale the discomfort out of your body through your breathing pores.

Close your eyes and practice this exercise until you are comfortable with it, then open your eyes and continue.

As you begin to sense some control of your distress through the breathing-level techniques, you can move to the next level—heaviness—to gain mastery over skeletal-muscle tension. Pain is usually made worse by unconscious bracing of these muscles.

This tension can usually be released by coupling your breathing with a muscle-tension contrast exercise, such as the one presented next in which you will intentionally make some of your muscles more tense, then release them to encourage the others to go out of spasm. As tension flows from muscles, they feel heavy.

Inhale a deep breath. Hold it. Simultaneously, tighten your toes. Tighten your fists. Push your tongue against the roof of your mouth. Hold. Now exhale as you drop your jaw, unclench your fists and loosen your toes. Feel the sensation of discomfort flow out of your body as your skeletal muscles become very loose and heavy.

Repeat this contrast exercise with your eyes closed until you begin to feel flowing heaviness as you exhale. Then open your eyes and go on reading.

The next level adds flowing warmth to body stability through an imaging process called the "warm blanket technique." The idea is that your mental elevator can move flowing warmth—warmth to soothe internal discomfort—to any region of your body where smooth muscles are tense or in spasm.

Curl the fingers of one hand into a loose fist and bring them to your slightly parted lips. As you breathe easy, deep, warm breaths, feel the sensation of warmth from your breath flowing into your hand to form the image of a small warm blanket.

Breathe easy, regular, warm breaths into your blanket/hand.

Continue breathing to expand the sensation of warmth in your hand.

When you sense that your hand is as warm as you can make it, slowly float your "warm blanket" to the back of your other hand, feeling its warmth begin to move slowly up your arm, to your shoulders, and now to your heart to encircle it with healing, quieting warmth.

Receive the soothing warmth of the blanket. As you breathe calm, regular breaths, expand the warming, safe sensations around your heart. Now imagine your heart pumping the warmth with each beat, sending it to the region of discomfort.

Close your eyes and repeat the exercise until you begin to actually feel the flowing warmth. Then open your eyes and continue.

Extend this exercise by bringing the warm blanket back to your curled fingers. Again breathe warm, regular breaths into your fingers, rewarming the "heating pad."

Now, while continuing to breathe into your curled fingers at your mouth to provide an ongoing source of heat, slowly, at about an inch per second, move the image of your heating pad slowly away from your fingers, along your arm, up through your upper arm, through your shoulders, and then gradually to any area of your body where you are experiencing pain or discomfort.

Direct the feeling of flowing warmth as you gently inhale and exhale to nourish and replenish the heating pad with its soothing warmth. Once the heating-pad image has become established and coupled with your breathing, gently move the hand that helped receive the warmth to cover the area of discomfort.

Now try a slightly different imaging technique for balancing distress with QR. Instead of moving the image of a small warm blanket to the region of discomfort, form the image of your "breathing pores" moving to that area. Breathe in clean fresh air through the pores to absorb the discomfort, then release the pain as little bubbles floating off into space as you breathe them out of the pores with a QR.

Once you can combine the levels of breathing, flowing heaviness and warmth, you should again find the six-second QR effective.

Close your eyes now and continue for a few minutes to see if you can move imagery easily from level to level, sensing release of tension and discomfort as you use QRs to create feelings of flowing heaviness and warmth wherever you choose to direct them with your breathing.

16. Session 8: Using QR in Daily Life

Begin this session by reviewing what you've covered so far, so that if any of the basic training elements are hazy in your mind, you can clear them up and then consolidate what you have learned.

You began by becoming aware of your tendency to respond to a need for alert *mental* activity by accidentally slipping your *body* into an unnecessary and uncomfortable passing-gear response.

Next you explored cues to the "manual" and "automatic" tension gearshift mechanisms of QR, particularly those involving your facial and breathing muscles. You began to use the QR Diary Scan to improve your awareness of early clues of inappropriate reactions to stress.

First separately, and then in combination, you explored QR exercises in breathing, heaviness and warmth.

161

Then you combined the Quieting Response with deepening exercises, using imagery—like the image of a mental movie screen—to emphasize that your alert mind can automatically choose the body tension level that fits the task at hand, that you needn't be at the mercy of an inappropriate passing-gear body.

Finally, you learned a "mental elevator" procedure for seeking an appropriate level at which to balance such physical distress as pain with the Quieting Response.

Throughout your training, you have envisioned yourself building a solidly grounded pyramid with the Quieting Reflex at its peak. Let's put this Quieting Reflex in perspective. It works over the long term, where "relaxation" or "meditation" techniques often fail, because:

1. It is grounded on sound physiological and psychological principles.

2. It does not require dropping out of an active life-style. Mere dropping out and relaxation may, like drugs, seriously impair alert, active mental performance and may create undesirable living patterns.

3. QR is an active skill that can be used all day long at the "scene of the crime" of stressful events. It is compatible with *all* behaviors—anywhere, any time.

4. Most importantly, QR provides just enough mental detachment so that your clever and alert mind can select the level of body response that will enrich rather than diminish your life experiences.

5. QRs are fun and self-rewarding. Once automatic, QR skills persist without practice.

One of QRs most powerful benefits is in preventive medicine, helping your body avoid stress illnesses without dependency on tranquilizing and other potentially addicting drugs.

In order to benefit optimally from QR, you need to make it automatic in your life. You want QR to automatically adjust your body machinery for balance while your mind remains active and alert.

To achieve this automatic capacity with QR, you must practice it consistently, just as you might practice typing without looking at the keyboard or driving a car. Building the QR pyramid is following the learning curve that over time will lead to real automaticity.

You have really just begun this learning process. You now know the basic QR exercises. You know the steps of the six-second Quieting Response. Now you must practice, practice, practice with *every* cue you encounter—every time a body scan reveals early signs of mounting tension, every time you catch yourself in a poor breathing pattern, every time the phone rings, every time something annoys or upsets you—as many as 50 to 100 times every day. Then a time will come when you sense with delight that a truly automatic QR has just occurred as a normal event in your body, without your awareness of a cue. The new "disguised" cue is an alteration in your basic breathing rhythm. This substitution of an unconscious cue for a conscious one—the transformation from the Quieting Response to the Quieting Reflex—can only occur with regular practice.

In addition to your ongoing daily practice of the Quieting Response, I suggest the following:

First, until your QR becomes automatic, promise yourself that every single night you will do a QR Diary Scan and then the QR Bedtime Daily Review as you lie in bed ready to fall asleep.

Second, whenever you feel physically ill, review and practice Session 7, Balancing Distress With QR, seeking the QR level that makes you feel better. This same session will help you recover the basic QR skills if you slip in your practice. Promise yourself now that you will spend time with Session 7 every time that you find that the six-second QR does not come easily or quickly.

Third, when you are in a private place, smiling a broad smile and letting your mouth fall open and your jaw drop as part of your QR provide marvelous sensations for reinforcing the response. But use discretion in practicing QR in public places. Smile inwardly, rather than breaking into a broad smile. Let your jaw, tongue and shoulders go loose in a subtle way, rather than opening your mouth and slouching your shoulders.

Right now, practice an exaggerated QR with a big smile, letting your mouth fall open with a jaw drop.

Now practice a subtle, inward QR, smiling inwardly and subtly permitting your jaw to go loose.

Let's review the deliberate Quieting Response. Then I will give you a better idea of what to expect when, with continued practice, you begin to experience the automatic Quieting *Reflex*.

The deliberate QR:

Cue: I am conscious of an annoyance, worry or tension. If I sense none, I do a "tongue thrust."

Response: I smile inwardly with my eyes and mouth.

I say to myself, "Alert mind, calm body."

I comfortably breathe in through my breathing pores.

I let my jaw, tongue and shoulders go loose, feeling a wave of heaviness and warmth flow to my toes as I exhale.

I resume normal activity with my mind alert and my body in proper gear. I attend to the cue that called forth my response with detachment, either resolving it with my mind or gearing up to deal with it with honest physical effort.

The following description gives some idea of the feelings you will experience with the automatic Quieting Reflex after continued practice. Observe your body response as you read.

The automatic QR:

Cue: My new cue is an unconscious alteration in normal, regular breathing. (Just now you may wish to briefly hold your breath in anticipation of this subtle cue.)

Automatic Reflex: I sense quiet delight and flowing heaviness and warmth in my body, coupled with an easy, regular breath. My alert mind automatically shifts my body into the proper gear to deal with whatever problem produced the cue.

We'll conclude this session by going through the steps of the QR Bedtime Daily Review once again:

Step 1: Rate today's activities on your QR Diary Scan.

Step 2: Lie down in bed with your eyes closed.

Step 3: Hold your hands in front of you as if you were praying. Take a deep breath, and holding it, press your hands together until you can feel your arm muscles begin to tremble. Maintain this trembling as long as you can, and then breathe out, letting your hands fall to your sides completely limp.

Step 4: Take another deep breath and hold it, slowly drawing your hands toward your face. When your hands touch your face, rest them there and breathe out, letting yourself go completely limp.

Step 5: Move your hands to lightly cup your mouth while you carry out quiet, easy breathing for about half a minute. Feel the warmth of your exhaled breath warming your hands and then flowing down your arms, spilling through your shoulders to flow through your whole body.

Step 6: As you sense flowing heaviness and warmth in your legs, permit your warm hands to slowly leave your mouth and rest on your abdomen or legs. Continue your quiet, easy breathing.

Step 7: With your eyes still closed, gently focus on an imaginary point just in front of the tip of your nose and imagine that your nose is leading you through a cloud of floating mist that fills your mind like a blank movie screen.

Step 8: Now, with your mind like a blank screen, conduct your daily review. See the activities of your day running backward on the screen, observing them without judgment unless an annoyance creeps in. If one does, dissolve it with a six-second QR and continue.

It is important that the QR technique become a truly automatic part of your behavior. Use the exercises as learning crutches—like the training wheels used to learn to ride a bicycle—to develop automatic QR skills that will be part of your life twenty-four hours a day.

17. Further Applications of QR

In chapters 4 and 5, I explained how stress can lead to a broad spectrum of physical and psychological problems. By ending the vicious cycle of chronic activation of the fight-or-flight response, QR has been effective in relieving a wide variety of difficulties, including many that have not been responsive to other treatments. QR's effectiveness in relieving a number of symptoms that are primarily physical in nature, such as migraine headache, tension headache, high blood pressure and stomach and bowel problems, has already been discussed. QR has also proven to be a workable technique for dealing with various conditions which, though they may include physical symptoms, center particularly on problems of psychological or mental tension.

Performance Anxiety

QR is highly effective in relieving anxieties. Musicians, dancers, athletes and public speakers have found it useful for dealing with performance anxiety, for example. In recent years, I have used QR to help a 41-year-old French-horn player with a major symphony orchestra.

Gordon used to become violently ill before every performance. He experienced an overwhelming emergency reaction in anticipation of performing—he'd become nauseated, throw up, develop terrible diarrhea, break out in cold sweats, shake and have trouble catching his breath. He was the "first chair" horn player—the one who usually performs featured solo parts—so his playing was often exposed. The French horn is a particularly difficult instrument, and though Gordon exhibited superb tone and technique during rehearsals, during performances he was constantly undermined by his anxiety. I happened to hear his orchestra on several occasions, and my own feeling was that his solos were the weakest part of their performances. He "blurbled" notes so frequently that I was surprised he was able to keep his first-chair position.

Gordon consulted many physicians and refused psychiatric referrals. After obtaining prescriptions from three doctors—none of whom knew of the others—he began taking 100 milligrams of Valium a day, although the limit approved by the Food and Drug Administration is 40 milligrams. The problem was, Gordon couldn't afford to just drop out, as the drug caused him to do; he needed to be sharp during performances. When you get up to 100 milligrams of Valium a day, the drug doesn't just tranquilize you; it dulls you.

Gordon came to see me after attending a summer French-horn workshop where I lectured on QR and stress regulation. I taught him the QR technique, and over the next six months, he noticed a remarkable improvement in his performances, as I did. But Gordon was slow to develop automaticity in the QR because he refused to give up his Valium, and the drug interrupts the very stress pathways that QR trains people to regulate. As a rule of thumb, we tell people who are taking 40 milligrams of Valium a day that it will take them twice as long to become automatic with QR—about a year, instead of six months.

Finally Gordon became frustrated; he felt that if he had to keep thinking about the steps of the QR, it would interfere with his playing. At that point, he slid into a new drug habit, obtaining Inderal, a "beta blocker" that is sometimes effective in relieving high blood pressure and also relieves anxiety in some people, like a tranquilizer. (Throughout the body, there are two types of receptors for adrenaline, termed alpha and beta. By occupying a beta receptor site, a "beta blocker" prevents adrenaline from activating the systems that normally respond to adrenaline.)

Gordon didn't like being dependent on drugs, but he was desperate. He felt his career was at stake, and he was willing to do anything to keep performing. In addition, he was one of a high percentage of the population that believes that such pills are more effective than QR-type skills, and it takes time to make a dent in that belief structure.

Although the FDA has made physicians more aware of the dangers of the minor tranquilizers, the use of Inderal to relieve anxiety is currently on the increase. Typically, however, the dosage has to be continually increased until the drug actually begins to make the patient ill. That's what happened to Gordon—he had to keep increasing his dosage until the Inderal made him nauseated and dizzy. Finally he came to see me again, and I withdrew him from the Inderal and started him back on the QR training. Now that he's in the program again—determined to stay with it this time until he develops the automatic Quieting Reflex—Gordon has become so enthusiastic that he's making plans for special QR workshops for musicians.

Tranquilizer Dependency

An even more serious case of tranquilizer dependency that I encountered also had its roots in performance anxiety. The patient, Janet, worked as a legal secretary. She was an extremely talented pianist and aspired to a concert career, but at 28, she had never performed in public, because she was too shy. As she dwelled on this problem, Janet's anxiety grew into a fear of going out in public at all, a condition psychiatrists call *agoraphobia*. If she was away from home and sensed any crowding by other people, she began to hyperventilate, broke out in a cold sweat, became nauseated and found herself unable to move. Frequently she had to be escorted by the police back to the safety of her apartment, and many times they took her to a hospital emergency room. Though Janet was an attractive young woman, dating was out of the question because of her overwhelming anxiety.

When Janet first came to see me, she told me that she was interested in learning QR, which she had heard me talk about on television. Over the course of the consultation, however, it became apparent that she was not so much interested in learning QR as in obtaining a prescription for Valium. Moreover, it wasn't difficult to tell that she must already be getting some Valium elsewhere. Finally I said to her, "You know, it sounds to me like you're burning the candle at both ends. If you don't get some real help with this problem, you're going to be in bad shape." She looked right at me. "Dr. Stroebel," she replied, "I didn't come here to learn your QR. I came here to get more candles."

At last I persuaded Janet that she had to find an alternative to tranquilizers to deal with her anxiety, because the amount she was already taking was making her so dull and depressed and disenchanted that she might become suicidal. High doses of Valium are a tremendous depressant. It wasn't until then that she acknowledged the full dimensions of her drug problem. She was seeing twelve different doctors, and each was prescribing Valium for her. She had built up to a habit of 400 milligrams a day—*ten times* the amount authorized by the FDA. She had been carefully filling each doctor's prescription with a different pharmacist so that neither the doctors nor the druggists would realize how much Valium she was getting. But her habit had rendered her almost incapable of playing the piano. She was sluggish and depressed and couldn't think clearly or coordinate her muscles very well.

To ease withdrawal from many drugs, doctors administer

what are called cross-tolerant drugs—drugs that affect some of the same body systems that are affected by the drug on which the person is dependent. Alcoholics are given Librium or Valium for a period of about ten days, for example, to keep them from developing DTs or having convulsions. Similarly, methadone is a cross-tolerant drug with heroin.

For the minor tranquilizers, however, there is no equivalent cross-tolerant drug. Alcohol might be a possibility, but it's not considered advisable to start a person on an alcohol habit to replace a Valium habit, especially since many tranquilizer-dependent people have what we call an "addiction-prone" personality. Consequently, withdrawal has to be carried out over a long period of time by gradually tapering off the tranquilizer dosage. Whereas an alcoholic or heroin addict might go through withdrawal in ten days with the aid of cross-tolerant drugs, Janet's withdrawal from Valium required three months of hospitalization.

After Janet's withdrawal was complete, I taught her QR, and she pursued the training avidly. Today, although she's continuing her career as a legal secretary, she has begun to perform in public. Several months ago I attended her performance of a Mozart piano concerto and was moved to tears by the fact that she had achieved such self-mastery. Janet's shyness about playing in public and her accelerating fear of leaving home have completely disappeared, and just recently she called to tell me she had become engaged to be married.

Hyperventilation

Hyperventilation, one of the manifestations of Janet's agoraphobia, is itself a widespread syndrome that responds very well to QR. Hyperventilation occurs when a person begins to overbreathe as part of the emergency response and then experiences a sense of panic. The standard medical treatment calls for susceptible people to carry a paper bag with them and hold it over nose and mouth and breathe into it when they begin to hyperventilate; the buildup of carbon dioxide in the bag usually stops the attack. Because QR emphasizes breathing, and the use of the QR Diary Scan increases the ability to determine the circumstances that trigger hyperventilation, QR has been most effective in helping people eliminate this problem.

Enhancing the Effectiveness of Other Therapies

The automaticity and brevity of the QR technique make it appropriate for yet another application, as a "transfer of training" device—a technique that enables people involved in psychotherapy, behavioral therapy, assertiveness training and similar modalities to be less dependent on their therapists and to transfer what they learn in therapy into real-life situations. What's at issue is something called "state-dependent learning," which is demonstrated in a classic experiment that's familiar to most psychology students. If a class is presented with lecture material in a single classroom, and then is randomly split in half, so that half the students take an exam in the room in which they were taught, and the other half in another room, the ones who take the exam in the room in which they learned the material will do much better than the ones in a new environment. The theory is that many aspects of that classroom learning setting are being related to the material learned in the course.

One would like to be able to generalize whatever is achieved in any therapeutic setting, such as a psychotherapeutic hour or a behavioral-modification hour, to every conceivable situation that a person might get himself into. But many patients confronted with emotional difficulties are able to maintain some stability only so long as their therapist is present or they're within the structured setting of a hospital or the therapist's office. When they get out in the real world, away from any connection with the place where they learned to gain control, they find it easy to slip out of control.

I recommend that QR be taught simultaneously with any therapeutic modality that's being applied. Because it will be practiced 50 to 100 times a day for six seconds, whenever the person is uptight or tense, the likelihood of the other therapeutic learning being associated with the QR and being used appropriately will be much greater. It's almost as though QR permits you to have a peripatetic therapeutic session going on twenty-four hours a day.

As an example, people undergoing a program of assertiveness training often experience a lot of stress within their bodies because they are normally passive and don't complain or argue even when they're becoming quite angry. If someone gets ahead of them in a supermarket line, for example, they just do a slow burn. QR is a useful adjunctive procedure to get them to practice their training, because at the very moment when they need to be assertive, the six-second QR, activated by the stress they experience, provides a productive pause that enables them to shift up and deal with the situation, rather than retreating into their passive pattern.

QR can be incorporated not only into psychotherapy, behavioral therapy, and assertiveness training, but into a variety of imagery procedures that therapists use for relaxation, desensitization to phobias, and consciousness expansion. Because QRs are brief and can be done anywhere and any time without arousing the attention of others, they can also be a valuable transfer mechanism when incorporated into more elaborate self-regulation procedures with potentially more far-reaching objectives, such as meditation systems, personal growth systems and various types of encounter groups and weekend retreats.

Substance Abuse

A number of people who have problems with alcoholism or obesity have been helped by using the six-second QR as a quick release valve or a pause for thinking before deciding to take a drink or eat a snack. It is important to note that the preferred treatment choice right now for these and similar problems is a group process like Alcoholics Anonymous. But if you are involved in a self-mastery program for weight control or to eliminate smoking, drinking or gambling, you can use QR to gain better long-term results.

Many of the group-support techniques for these problems—including those of Alcoholics Anonymous, Gamblers Anonymous and Weight Watchers—work initially when you are highly motivated, but lose effectiveness over time, especially if you lose touch with your teacher, coach or group. QR is unique in that it is automatic, it persists over time and it occurs at the very scene of whatever habits need to be changed. A QR used at the moment of temptation—when you have an urge to snack, smoke or drink—is a quick urge relief valve. By reducing your body tension arousal level, the six-second pause can interrupt your craving and boost your willpower.

Among the 1200 people who have gone through the QR training under my supervision have been many who were addicted to narcotics or alcohol, and we've seen improvements in their life-styles because they could use the quick QR technique right at the time they were feeling the pressure of their addiction. Leon, who had been a member of Alcoholics Anonymous for ten years—and who had slipped "off the wagon" seven times in that period—came to me to learn the QR technique to gain control over his muscle-contraction headaches. He found the QR remarkably effective in helping him resist urges—usually experienced when he is frustrated or feeling pressure at work or at home—to stop at a bar or skip an AA meeting.

A number of investigators are now studying the use of QR training in conjunction with the other elements of established group-support systems for relief of substance abuse problems. Pending completion of these studies, you should incorporate QR as a quick reminder technique under supervision of trained group leaders who can relate it to the overall philosophy and framework of the group's program.

Obsessions, Compulsions and Creativity

QR has also proven to be very helpful in relieving obsessive-compulsive behavior, which people manifest when they feel compelled to ruminate, repeat and carry out unproductive ritualistic behaviors. Examples include compulsive hand washing or fear of stepping on a crack in the sidewalk. By encouraging a smile and an alert mind, QR teaches people trapped in such patterns that they can "hang loose" and that life should be fun.

People in creative fields have found QR to be remarkably effective in dealing with various "blocks," such as writer's block, which is precipitated when one is obsessed with perfection and feels one has to get written material down perfectly the very first time. The mind is very clever at developing rationalizations and getting more and more grim as a deadline approaches. Many people who write have found QR—particularly in its aspect of amused detachment—to be enormously useful in helping them realize that they just have to get their material down on paper—the world isn't going to end tomorrow, and they'll be able to shape and revise their writing once they've recorded the main ideas.

Many people have found QR to be a wonderful starting point in programs for personal growth and increasing innate potentials. Freed from the demands of a body constantly locked into passing gear, one's alert and clever mind has a new perspective for personal growth, self-mastery and self-actualization.

Now there is exciting evidence, though we don't have proof of it yet, that QR can actually enhance creativity. At the heart of this speculation is basic research on the specialization of function of the left and right halves of the brain. Roger Sperry, Ph.D., of the California Institute of Technology, received the Nobel Prize for 1981 for this work, which has been popularized in Betty Edward's *Drawing on the Right Side of the Brain.* Sperry's findings imply that stressed people tend to overactivate the left side of the brain, which is involved with language function and logic and all things that seem to make us winners in the world, and to underuse the right brain, which is involved with more creative functioning and synthesis—getting the "big picture." Stress is thought to be a left-brain function overdriving the body. Studies now in progress suggest that the six-second QR pause briefly slows left-brain functioning to permit access to the right brain. QR, then, may represent a new path for utilizing the full potential of our unique human mental capacities.

18. Reading, 'Riting 'Rithmetic—and the Fourth "R," QR

Many adults who have learned the six-second QR technique have asked whether the procedure might be adapted to help children and adolescents deal with an increasingly stressful world in which many young people seem to be turning to drug abuse or losing joyous interest in life at an earlier and earlier age. When children experience stress as the result of projected adult anxieties or a sense of low self-esteem, they often manifest it in "acting-out" behavior or withdrawal. Discipline in our schools has become a major problem that seriously interferes with the educational process and is one factor leading to many teachers retiring because of "teacher burnout."

I can remember my parents and teachers telling me when I was growing up that I would get sick if I didn't relax, nap and slow down to save my energy for efforts that really needed it.

This parental advice was very much on my mind when I did get sick or had a terrible day.

Like most kids, I worried a lot—about my appearance, about my performance in school, about making my parents angry and about my status among my peers. I worried about my worries and, in retrospect, that made everything worse. Although I know better today, I privately thought that I was the only person with such worries. But adults who told me to stop worrying never told me how to do it, and I wasn't even sure I wanted to "relax," because I had so much zest and curiosity about my world that I feared I might miss something.

An Inborn Quieting Capacity

The feelings of pressure that I experienced when I was younger suggest that QR may be an answer to "how" young people can relax. When I developed the QR concept in 1974, I was dealing with a clinic population ranging in age from 7 to 70, and I was astounded at the ease with which youngsters acquired the QR skill. Older patients found it more difficult to develop the skill and particularly to transfer it into the "real world" with its inevitable stress and worries. Despite the faster rate at which children are forced to grow up today, my colleagues and I believe that because children have not experienced the calling forth of the emergency response as often as adults, it's not as practiced and ingrained a tendency in them.

It is our experience with children that first led us to believe that the Quieting Reflex, like the emergency response, is an inborn trait. Studies are currently being conducted to determine if this is indeed so. Young children seem to adapt happily, with very few stress-related problems, until they encounter the discipline, confinement and pressure of parental expectations that accompany starting school at the age of 5 or 6. This fact lends credence to the idea that the Quieting Reflex is inherent at birth and is only extinguished or overwhelmed as children encounter the frequent arousal and stress levels of classroom life. When children do begin to experience such tension, their physiological responses are identical to those of adults, and children have less choice than adults in avoiding stressful situations.

Quieting for Children

In 1977, with these points in mind, I consulted with Margaret Holland and my wife, Elizabeth Stroebel, both of whom have extensive teaching experience, about the possibility of including a fourth "R"—QR—in the education of children. Wouldn't it be remarkable if we could help youngsters maintain the QR capability and recognize it as an important life skill that could spare them from being overwhelmed by the fight-or-flight mechanism?

Subsequently a program, *Kiddie QR*, was written. The goals of this program parallel the aims of the basic QR program— to give youngsters the ability to discriminate among body tension states, and to teach them how to reverse the physiological changes that occur when the emergency response is called up unnecessarily. The format of this audio-cassette program is designed for easy use in the classroom, by parents as a family activity, or by health-care professionals in clinical settings.

Kiddie QR, prepared by Elizabeth for ages 3 through 9, divides the QR technique into sixteen brief—four to seven minute—experiential exercises, easily integrated into classroom use or dental and pediatric settings without serious interruption of the routine at hand. This program uses different images to accomplish some of the things accomplished by the adult program, but always with the same physiological objective—to develop a hierarchy of behavior that is incompatible with the emergency response.

QR's "Body Friends"

QR is presented as a friend who lives inside your body along with many other symbolically named body characters. Some of these characters, like "Rigid Robot" and "Fighty Fists," represent faulty-bracing states seen in tense children. Recognizing "Body Bike Cycle" and "Grouchy Head" helps kids deal with hyperactivity. Other body characters represent helpful elements of the QR training. The program emphasizes that you can choose the right friends for the situation at hand.

The concept presented in the adult program as "breathing pores" in the bottoms of the feet is taught to children as "magic breathing holes." Discrimination of facial tension and the jaw drop is accomplished by an imaginary "magic jaw string" tied to the chin that can be used to slowly pull the jaw down. The little ones learn about the temporomandibular joint, which they call "Mr. TMJ," and they go on "finger trips" to locate it. They learn the words "dysponesis" and "homeostasis"—the latter described as "My Very Own Good-Feeling Self"—and they love to use these big words in the hopes that an adult will ask, "What does that mean?" Then on they go to describe it in their own terms. The children also learn to take a "*D and W*," or "dysponesis watch," when they're riding in a car. When they look out the window and see adult drivers exhibiting passing-gear emergency responses as they sit in traffic, the kids often giggle and say that if the people were doing their QRs, they wouldn't be so tense.

Kiddie QR teaches children to pause and discriminate body arousal states. They learn that they're in control—that they can interrupt the fight-or-flight response and shift body gears before difficult tasks, unpleasant situations or fights overtake their bodies. Because many children think that adults don't worry about things, they are also taught that fears and worries are normal in adults. They learn that it's okay to have worries, but also that their sixteen "body friends" can help them deal with these worries. With these friends, the children learn how to build a "Healthy, Happy Body," developing coping strategies to integrate negative stressful aspects of their lives with the positive stresses experienced by all healthy individuals.

Defusing Tense Situations

Kiddie QR provides a marvelous means for dealing with tense situations between adult and child. When a child is unruly, a parent or teacher usually confronts him, and often the result is counterproductive. With these programs, instead of putting a child down, the adult says, "Let's do a QR together." With the emotion of the situation defused, child and adult can then intelligently discuss what might have been better ways of coping with whatever precipitated the tension.

Suitability for School Use

Although contemporary educators are aware of and concerned about stress management, many "relaxation" programs have been rejected by schools because they don't work well in the classroom. In addition, some stress-management programs for use in schools seem to threaten the belief structure of many families. Some forms of meditation, for example, are opposed by parent groups because members believe they represent a religious position other than their own. QR, as a quick, scientifically based technique that can be used "at the scene of the crime" of stress, surmounts these difficulties. It does not involve psychotherapy or infringe on parental beliefs.

Controlled studies have demonstrated that *Kiddie QR* is remarkably effective in classroom and clinical settings. The theory that children seem to learn QR much more quickly than adults has been borne out by these studies, which strongly suggest that QR should be taught at an early stage in education to help youngsters avoid some of the stress-related illnesses that can be expected to become increasingly common as they grow older.

To observe an elementary-school classroom before and after

the introduction of *Kiddie QR* is like witnessing a miracle. I have seen "before" classrooms in which the teacher has to scream frequently during the day in order to maintain quiet and discipline. She is constantly confronted with a bunch of wiggly little minds and bodies. After the children learn QR—which takes only sixteen to twenty days—the teacher, instead of screaming when they become rambunctious, simply says, "Now let's all do a QR." Suddenly a hush falls over the classroom. All the little faces break into smiles, and you can see the kids take in breaths through their "magic breathing holes," drop their jaws and slump their shoulders. Six seconds after asking for the QR, the teacher has thirty creative, active, alert, wiggly little minds—with "dewiggled" bodies. This is the concept of an alert Type A mind and a calm Type B body.

Kiddie QR has been introduced in both public- and private-school systems, and the *Kiddie QR* program is already being used by well over half a million children. The cost of these programs is very low—less than one cent per student—because an audio-cassette package passed through a school system can service thousands of kids per year. Usually the teacher plays the cassettes in the classroom, though transcripts are provided for the teacher who wants to present the material personally. Teachers can learn the program from the package alone, but it helps to have three or four hours of inservice training, and many will benefit from reading this book.

Many teachers, once they have been exposed to *Kiddie QR*, want to learn adult QR. In other cases, educators have first been introduced to adult QR in stress-management programs for teachers; when the programs for student populations were developed, these were initially among the most enthusiastic users. In Mesa, Arizona, for example, the thirty-four clinical psychologists in the 40,000-student system first began using QR themselves. They have now implemented both student programs.

Easing the Trials of Special-Needs Children

We are now working with special-needs children—children with physical handicaps, learning difficulties or emotional problems—exploring ways that special-education teachers, working with a smaller teacher-student ratio, can use these programs. QR is marvelous for interrupting the tendency to try too hard that goes on with all kinds of physical therapies. Most stutterers, for example, have been told for years and years to relax, but usually the more they try to relax the more they stutter. By breaking such cycles, QR can greatly accelerate the education of special-needs children. Pediatricians and child psychologists are also using QR with children exhibiting such stress-related symptoms as migraines, high blood pressure and stomach disturbances.

"Kiddie QR" for the Aging

Another application of the *Kiddie QR* program is its use, recently being explored, in geriatric facilities. A lot of the images and vocabulary that appeal to children also appeal to aging people whose mental abilities have become somewhat impaired. After undertaking the training, these people begin to kid one another—pointing out signs of "Fighty Fists" or "Rigid Robot"—and this noticeably improves their adjustment to the difficulties of growing older.

Quieting for Life

The importance of the QR programs for children and young people can best be summarized by an excerpt from a report on education perspectives in 1981 published by the National Education Association of the United States. In a chapter entitled "Stress Management Education," Dr. Marigold Edwards wrote,

> What can the average classroom teacher do? Time is limited. The curriculum is already crowded. No money is available for equipment. The teacher has no special training. One answer to these and other problems of teaching stress management in the school setting is the Quieting Reflex programs developed by [the Stroebels] . . . The *Kiddie QR* for ages three to nine . . . consists of sequential exercises that follow the physiological principles of the Quieting Response and Reflex in operable language consistent with the youngsters' age and state of development. The objective is to teach children this skill, the Quieting Reflex, for life, or to help the child "dewiggle" the body but wiggle his marvelous mind.

Enhancing Their Future

My interest in developing QR programs for children is a reflection of my continuing enthusiasm for the QR technique, as an individual who has benefited from it personally, and as a professional who has seen it help so many other people. QR has been so gratifying to me that I'm committing a major part of the rest of my professional life to helping the QR concept to be taught to virtually every child in elementary school. I want to reach children *before* they begin developing problems. It's exciting to consider the possibility of a future population that will not suffer from the stress-related illnesses that account for the overwhelming majority of modern medical complaints.

Even more intriguing than the possibility of a generation that is free of this physical suffering is the possibility of a generation that enjoys the full benefits of enhanced creativity. In the last chapter, I explained how QR, by permitting increased access to the right brain, may open up new vistas for utilizing the complete potential of our unique human mental capacities.

In 1906, long before research into "brain lateralization" was undertaken, the famous psychologist William James sensed the existence of this untapped power of the mind. He was writing about yoga, but his thoughts pertain to QR as well:

> I wonder whether the . . . discipline may not be, after all, in all its phases, simply a methodical way of waking up deeper levels of willpower than are habitually used, and thereby increasing the individual's vital tone and energy. I have no doubt whatever that most people live, whether physically, intellectually or morally, in a very restricted circle of their potential being. They make use of a very small portion of their possible consciousness, and of their soul's resources in general, much like a man who, out of his whole bodily organism, should get into the habit of using and moving only his little finger. Great emergencies and crises show us how much greater our vital resources are than we had supposed.*

Enhancing Your Present

What might your potentials be? If you only use a small part of your mental capacity now, and could increase the capacity you use by getting out of unnecessary passing gear, it might mean a doubling of your productivity as a thinker. Or even better, doubling of your appreciation of life and the world around you.

As people get into excessive Type A behavior and emphasize thinking, logic and getting ahead in life, they narrow their focus so that they miss much of what is going on around them and don't really have much fun in their lives. When they renounce the tyranny of a passing-gear body, many things that they have bypassed because of the pressure of running from job to job and appointment to appointment begin to interest them again. When people give up their straight-ahead focus and become aware of the richness around them, their worlds expand enormously. Just walking along the street becomes a glorious experience. Regardless of your chronological age, QR requires

*The Letters of William James, ed. H. James (Boston: Atlantic Monthly Press, 1920), vol. 2, pp. 253–4.

a few hours of pleasurable learning activity that can not only relieve a variety of physical and psychological symptoms, but can reawaken your childlike wonder at all that is beautiful in the world.

Suggestions
for Further Reading

Benson, Herbert. *The Relaxation Response*. New York: William
    Morrow, 1973.
    Presents a fairly systematic overview of meditation, as well
    as a secularized version of the Transcendental Meditation
    technique.

Carrington, Patricia. *Clinically Standardized Meditation*. Kendall
    Park, N.J.: Pace Books, 1978.

————.*Freedom in Meditation*. New York: Anchor Press, 1977.
Presents the rationale and a second secularized version of Transcendental Meditation.

Cousins, Norman. *Anatomy of an Illness as Perceived by the
    Patient*. New York: W. W. Norton, 1979.
    A widely respected past editor of *The Saturday Review
    of Literature* describes how mental attitude and a sense of
    humor were essential for his recovery from a severe illness.

Friedman, Meyer, and R. H. Rosenman. *Type A Behavior and Your Heart*. Greenwich, Ct.: Fawcett Crest, 1974.
An early and definitive book describing the Type A behavior pattern which increases tendency toward heart attacks.

Goldwag, Elliott M., ed. *Inner Balance: The Power of Holistic Healing*. Englewood Cliffs, N.J.: Prentice-Hall, Inc., 1979.
A collection of outstanding chapters on maintaining body self-regulation, by authors such as Selye, Simonton, Jampolsky, Kubler-Ross and Stroebel.

Gordon, Barbara. *I'm Dancing as Fast as I Can*. New York: Harper & Row, 1979.
A fascinating but tragic account of a highly creative person's dependence on and problems with minor tranquilizers in dealing with stress.

Green, Elmer, and A. Green. *Beyond Biofeedback*. New York: Delacorte, 1977.
A popular book relating biofeedback mechanisms, self-regulation, and meditation by two pioneers in the field of biofeedback from the Menninger Foundation.

Jacobson, E. *You Must Relax*. New York: McGraw-Hill, 1978.
The definitive, popular book describing the procedures of progressive relaxation.

Jencks, Beata. *Your Body: Biofeedback at its Best*. Chicago: Nelson Hall, 1977.
An outstanding book relating the concepts of biofeedback to different exercises in increasing body awareness, to reduce stress-related problems.

Lamott, K. *Escape From Stress*. New York: G. P. Putnam's Sons, 1975.
An excellent overview of the causes and effects of stress, this surveys numerous self-regulation techniques for relieving and avoiding the ravages of disorders and diseases related to stress.

Pelletier, K. R. *Mind as Healer, Mind as Slayer*. New York: Delta, 1977.
Presents a superb overview of how we can use our minds to produce illness as well as to help our bodies heal.

Selye, Hans. *The Stress of Life*. New York: McGraw-Hill, 1951.
   The first popular book on stress published by the real pioneer
   in the field.

————.*Stress Without Distress*. Philadelphia: J. B. Lippincott,
   1974.
   This popular book describes how some stress is crucial for
   healthy, productive behavior.

Stroebel, Charles F. *Quieting Response Training*. New York:
   BioMonitoring Applications Publications, 1978.
   This is an audio cassette-instruction manual program which
   has set forth many of the ideas which are refined in the
   present book.

Whatmore, George B., and D. R. Kohli. "Dyspnonesis: A Neu-
   rophysiologic Factor in Functional Disorders." In Peper,
   Erik, et al., eds. *Mind/Body Integration*. New York: Plenum
   Press, 1979.
   Contains many interesting chapters culled from the work on
   self-regulation over the last ten years and has an especially
   good chapter on the concept of dysponesis, as frequently
   referred to in this book.

242